Fairies, Pookas, and Changelings

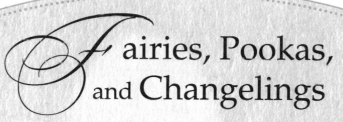

Fairies, Pookas, and Changelings

A Complete Guide to the Wild and Wicked Enchanted Realm

VARLA VENTURA

WEISER BOOKS

This edition first published in 2017 by Weiser Books, an imprint of
Red Wheel/Weiser, LLC
With offices at:
65 Parker Street, Suite 7
Newburyport, MA 01950
www.redwheelweiser.com

ISBN: 978-1-57863-611-2

Library of Congress Cataloging-in-Publication Data available upon request

Cover design by Jim Warner
Cover photograph © Album/Florilegius/Superstock
Interior by Deborah Dutton
Typeset in Palatino LT Std and Bickham Script Std

Printed in the United States of America
M&G

10 9 8 7 6 5 4 3 2 1

*To my mother, who taught me
the true art of the fairy tale.*

Contents

Chapter 2

The Hand That Rocks the Cradle: Changelings and Other Greedy Kidnappers of the Fairy Kingdom 95

Chapter 3

I'm Not Drunk, It's Just My Pooka: Tales of the Trickster Fairy and Its Wild Counterparts

Chapter 4

Is That All There Is? Fairies Who Give, or the Barter System

Chapter 5

Introduction
The Woods Are Lovely, Dark, and Deep

If you are usually a fearful person who likes to barricade your door and hunker beneath the bedclothes each night, worried about what might rattle the locks or slip through the cracks, you should not undertake to read the book that follows this introduction. Many of the stories in this book harken back to a different era: one without the niceties of today. A time when most homes did not have electricity, when candlelight failed to chase away all the night shadows, horses were the main mode of transport, and the fairies and goblins of olde still roamed the earth in large numbers. Today, we can leave a night-light on or we can listen to the soothing sounds of ocean waves on our iPods to lull us to sleep. We fear burglars or worse; our nightly news is more terrifying than some gentle old tale. Or is it? If you think fairies are merely delicate beings that follow you about on gossamer wings, you are in for quite a shock: the <u>Kingdom of the Fairy is one of vengeance,</u> thievery, trickery, and wild creatures who wish nothing more than to steal your child, drown you in the bog, or spoil your best Sunday shoes. The woods are lovely, dark, and deep. You have been warned.

Before we head deeper into the shadowy forests and craggy caves of the Fairy Kingdom, I should begin by explaining what I am referring to when I say fairy. The Irish or Gaelic word for fairy is *sidheóg* or *sidhe* (shee). The *bean-sidh* (bahn-shee) is a wild and fearsome member of the fairy kingdom signified by her mourning-like wail, but can also refer to any female fairy spirit, and *daoine sidhe* (deenee-shee) can be any fairy creature. The Dutch, German, and French words are all similar: *fée*. In Russian, the phonetic translation is *feya*, and in Italian or Latin it's *fata*, all of which give root to the modern word for fairy, faerie, and fae. They are known as the good people, the little people, the wee folk. Around the world there are terms for magical beings who dwell in a land not far, far away, but rather one that coexists or overlaps with our "regular" world. Fairyland. It can be accessed on purpose by witches and seers, on accident by drunken fools, and without effort by children. Fairies can be called upon to help as they can be implored to bring harm. Their trickery is legendary and perhaps this is the origin of the phrase, "Be careful what you wish for."

Within the domain of fairies one might find all manner of loathsome, fearsome, or irresistibly naughty beings. They love to test human nature. Hobgoblins, sprites, bogeys, pixies, changelings, pookas, goblins, bonga, duende, and elves all dwell in the Kingdom of the Fairy.

They creep about at crossroads, they hide beneath leaves. They are the twig-snap behind you on a walk in a moonlit forest, the rattle at the window that you only hope is just the wind.

They creep about at crossroads, they hide beneath leaves.
They are the twig-snap behind you on a walk in a moonlit forest, the rattle at the window that you only hope is just the wind.

They are seen with a drunken eye and with a sober nod, a fit of laughter and a scream of terror. The hobgoblin will clean your house for a saucer of milk, but the banshee will destroy every cup and saucer in your cupboard with a vengeance stronger than a hurricane.

William Butler Yeats classified Irish fairies into two types: solitary and sociable. Among the sociable were the merrow (merfolk) and "the Sheoques" who live and "haunt the sacred thorn bushes and green raths." The solitary list is much longer, and includes the leprechaun, pooka, and banshee, among others.

In this book I attempt to explore just some of the different kinds of fairies. Yea, though I've slept many a night near a fairy mound and cavorted with creatures great and small, I by no means purport to be the authority on all the tenants of Fairyland. In my travels, far and wide, peering under rocks and jumping at shadows, I've learned one thing for certain: no matter your breadth of knowledge or preparedness, when entering the realm of the fairy there are always—always—surprises.

The pursuit of the fae is a difficult quest to end. In truth, it never ends.

The scholar, the poet, and the magician alike can spend a lifetime seeking out these magical creatures and proof of their existence, only to be thwarted by the breaking of the dawn.

Just as the ghost hunter seeks to catch something on film, to bring home evidence of a haunting, so too the fairy seeker wishes to prove they are not mad because they keep hearing voices in the garden. And yet, the true knowledge comes at a price, perhaps too dear for some.

As William Butler Yeats wrote in the introduction to his *Fairy and Folk Tales of the Irish Peasantry*:

The scholar, the poet, and the magician alike can spend a lifetime seeking out these magical creatures and proof of their existence, only to be thwarted by the breaking of the dawn.

> The old women are most learned, but will not so readily be got to talk, for the fairies are very secretive, and much resent being talked of; and are there not many stories of old women who were nearly pinched into their graves or numbed with fairy blasts?

Remember too that in the rural parts of England and Wales, as well as Ireland, the people were not so removed from what now are thought to be mere stories. Though cynicism was setting in (you can detect notes of it throughout Yeats's works), many people lived their

daily lives with a certain understanding and apprecia-
tion of the other realms. So these stories straddle the
world of the invisible and the visible, the known and
the unknown.

The feverish search that overtakes the fairy seeker
can be viewed as a gift from the fae themselves. The
lines between real and imagined, visible and
invisible (lines that many of you must
know are already threadbare for the
likes of me) become worn away. This
is the trick of the fairy, the enticements
and enchantments. The bewitching. You lose
yourself, you lose track of time. And while I
do not wish you sleepless nights, a-huntin'
through the forests of the north, it is my
hope that by reading this book you will
be transported, if only for a few minutes,
to another realm. That you will become lost among the
stories and give in to the grand question of what if?
That you will chuckle, perhaps cringe, and, surely, at
least once, shiver.

If, however, you find yourself scoffing in disbelief
with every page, I can only suggest this: watch your
back, for you are being watched. Be careful how much

you drink, measure your steps home carefully, and always walk fast at night. Walk quickly over streams and double-bolt your doors. Because even the turn of the page is an invitation to believe, and from there you have no choice but to run.

VARLA VENTURA
THE NORTH WOODS, 2016

Chapter 1

A Fear of Little Men

*Elves, Trolls, Leprechauns, Tree Spirits,
Brownies, Coblyns, Dwarves, Goblins,
Bonga, Trolls, and Other Fairy Folk
of Glen, Forests, and Hearth*

*When hunting in the morning dawn
Or through the dead of night
Be careful of the winding path
That is lit by fairy light*

—CAMERON BUMBERFORD, "A HUNTER'S PARADISE"

Once upon a time, goblins, brownies, and elves were as common in a household as a bar of soap or a scrub bucket. While few families set out to lure these domestic fairy folk (they saved their trapping skills for the leprechaun and his infamous golden store), most accepted their presence (or at least blamed the good people for messes, missing objects, and crying babies) and the unwritten rules that went along with housing such a creature. Leave a dish of milk out, sweep your own hearth, don't lock the cupboards up. The world of the domestic fairy was the most common to overlap with that of the mortal. Today we are more likely to blame ghosts than we are fairy folk. And yet who among us has not lost a sock or a watch, a favorite earring or important document, sure that it had been put away for safekeeping? And yet we never point to fairies as the culprits. Instead we blame our own busyness, or absentmindedness, or habit of housecleaning while drunk.

I ask you this: can you say for certain that when you wake up in the morning everything is *exactly* as you left it? Nothing is out of place? I think it is reasonable to assume that many of us do not do a thorough inspection of our homes the night before (if you are in this habit, please text me your number because my house wants for ordering). So if something is slightly awry in the morning, we may not notice it, in particular if we have children in the home. This, my dear ones, is how it begins. A penknife here, a dollar bill there, and that oh-so-mild feeling of being watched. But do not fear too much. As you read on, you will hopefully find the information that follows not only entertaining but useful, should things suddenly (or gradually) begin to go amiss in your household.

When it comes to the woodland dwellers, the range of fairy personalities is bipolar at best. From reclusive and angry to taunting and tricky, even among the different classes of fairies variety seems to be the one consistency. With the exception of the rather solitary leprechaun, some elves, pixies, gnomes, dwarves, goblins, and the like seem to almost crave human attention. Other folkish imps wish nothing more than to banish all humans from ever crossing their paths, or to destroy our happiness, or trap us to a life of servitude, or create mayhem and, as a result, possible death.

Should you walk through fairylight (twilight) on a midsummer's eve, humming quietly to yourself as the frogs croon and the bats venture out, you just might meet some of the fellows in this chapter.

Should you walk through fairylight (twilight) on a midsummer's eve, humming quietly to yourself as the frogs croon and the bats venture out, you just might meet some of the fellows in this chapter.

From hedgerow to hearth to mushroomy glen, venture on and into the sylvan world of the fairy.

Elves

Just as there are dozens of variations on the word fairy, there are just as many beings called elves. In some stories, the terms are used interchangeably, and pixies get into the mix to boot. Perhaps this is because, no matter how many volumes of folklore we comb through, no matter how many fairy songs we think we hear on a Midsummer's Eve, fairy folk are far too difficult to classify with any absolute categories. What is a pixie in one part of the world may be a forest spirit in another; an elf

becomes more goblinish when described by a certain old timer who recounts days of youthful encounters.

Still, it is common enough to imagine elves, thanks to our widespread belief in one Santa Claus, as helpful little fellows, not much higher than a grown man's knee, that know all manner of cunning ways and talents. In some places, Santa Claus himself is considered an elf or magical being. Today's elf wears striped socks and does a silly dance, or watches over your kids to make sure they are good in the days leading up to Christmas (occasionally in the form of a stalkerish doll). Most accounts agree that bands of elves usually have a king and queen, always at least an Elf King.

Ellyllon is the term used throughout Wales for smallish elves who hang out in groves and valleys. The ellyllon pal around with English elves, too. Both types are described as both angelic and devilish, helpful and mischievous. They dine on toadstools or other poisonous mushrooms and _ymenyn tylwyth teg_, aka fairy butter, aka a kind of butter-like fungus that grows deep in the crevices of limestone. The Welsh variety wear foxglove flowers as their own gloves. Foxglove, or digitalis, is a powerful and toxic plant that has been used as a sedative for many years (someone should have alerted Joey Ramone). It is used in modern medicine to treat congestive heart failure. It is not surprising, then, that fungus and foxglove have otherworldly associations (or is it simply that the fae have left their magic in these plants?).

In Scandinavia, especially Sweden, the elves are beautiful and mostly peaceful creatures called *Alvheim* or sometimes *alve*, *alv*, *alb*, or *elbe*. In Norway, elves are known as *Huldrafolk*. They live underground in hilly and rocky areas. Their music is irresistible but always in a minor key and very mournful. In Italy, the *Linchetti* are nocturnal elves who dislike disorder and cause nightmares to those with messy rooms (*Giovanni! Clean your room!*). *Gianes* are Italian forest elves, who can prophesize the future and are adept at weaving.

In Thomas Keightley's 1892 volume, *The Fairy Mythology*, he shares this story from Denmark lore:

> The Danish peasantry give the following account of their Ellefolk or Elve-people. The Elle-people live in the Elle-moors. The appearance of the man is that of an old man with a

low-crowned hat on his head; the Elle-woman is young and of a fair and attractive countenance, but behind she is hollow like a dough-trough. Young men should be especially on their guard against her, for it is very difficult to resist her; and she has, moreover, a stringed instrument, which, when she plays on it, quite ravishes their hearts. The man may be often seen near the Elle-moors, bathing himself in the sunbeams, but if anyone comes too near him, he opens his mouth wide and breathes upon them, and his breath produces sickness and pestilence. But the women are most frequently to be seen by moonshine; then they dance their rounds in the high grass so lightly and so gracefully, that they seldom meet a denial when they offer their hand to a rash young man.

In Praise of Legolas

Who can think of elves today and not pay homage to J. R. R. Tolkien's world described in his three-volume novel, *The Lord of the Rings*. Elrond, Arwen, and Galadriel are all primary elf characters, but few can compare to Legolas, now made infamous as played by Orlando Bloom in the Peter Jackson movies. Like his cohorts, he prefers to coexist with humans (but dislikes dwarves). Tolkien is said to have borrowed extensively from mythology, especially that of the Norse, when imagining his world.

The Scandinavian Christmas Troll

What young child doesn't love the din of Christmas? The lights in shop windows and holiday hum, a promise of bellies full of cookies and piles of presents. And when most of us think of Christmas, we think of a bearded man in a red suit, jolly, and adept at delivering toys. We accept his magical elfin assistants and flying abilities in a way that goes almost unquestioned, chalking it up to the "magic of the season." And when we think of holiday horrors, it is usually high prices or forgotten presents, perhaps a burnt Christmas ham.

What would your children say if you whispered tales to them not of Christmas cheer and sightings of the elusive Santa Claus, but stories of a different kind of magic altogether? What if you told them that at the stroke of midnight on Christmas Eve, curious things happen: Wells run with blood. Animals talk. Buried treasures are revealed and water turns to wine. And if you warned them of witches that leapt from roof to roof, or ghosts that hung about the chimneys waiting

to visit them in the dark of the night, would they still anticipate the winter holidays in the same way?

Early twentieth-century author Clement A. Miles was a historian and an amateur anthropologist of sorts. His 1912 collection *Christmas in Ritual and Tradition, Christian and Pagan* is not just a cross-cultural look at the origins of Santa Claus. Here you will find werewolves, bogeys, and trolls. You will find curses and hexes and imminent death, rituals of the dead, and goblin offerings. You will be warned of the devil and cautioned against laziness.

Beware the Scandinavian Christmas Trolls! They love to dance and drink through the night on Christmas Eve. If you are in Bavaria, take heed of the *Berchte*—a wretched bogey who cuts open the stomachs of naughty children. And at all costs, do not walk outside alone should you ever find yourself in Greece during the Twelve Days of Christmas. For there lurks the most horrid beast of all: the *Kallikantzaroi* or *Karkantzaroi*, a horrid half-human, half-animal monstrosity that plays tricks and ravages households, often leaving the occupants dead. Some say it is a mortal man transformed into a beastly creature, others say it is manifested from the supernatural beyond.

Miles writes:

In the Scandinavian countries simple folk have a vivid sense of the nearness of the supernatural on Christmas Eve. On Yule night no one should go out, for he may meet uncanny beings of all kinds. In Sweden the Trolls are believed to celebrate Christmas Eve with dancing and revelry. "On the heaths, witches and little Trolls ride, one on a wolf, another on a broom or a shovel, to their assemblies, where they dance under their stones . . . In the mount are then to be heard mirth and music, dancing and drinking. On Christmas morn, during the time between cock-crowing and daybreak, it is highly dangerous to be abroad . . ."

Red Hat Clapping

The signature red hat of Santa Claus is often likened to the red-capped mushroom of the forest and the many little men who share the look. Gnomes, whose domain is woods and gardens and who look after crops and children, are often seen wearing red hats. Even the leprechaun, whom we know today as sporting a top hat or green bowler, once wore a red cap.

Shoe Me the Money

Leprechauns are also known by more than pots of gold in the Fairy Kingdom. The leprechaun can be identified by the sound of his knocking or tap-tap-tapping upon his little shoe bench, as they are cobblers and the sound is that of their tiny hammers making elfin shoes. Fairies prize shoes and fine clothes far more than gold. If you can trap a leprechaun—some say green velvet and fine wine do the trick—the location of all that hidden gold could be revealed. But be aware that simply looking away from the 'chaun for a moment can allow them to vanish back into the green grass or woods where you happened upon them. The leprechaun is believed to be a perpetual bachelor elf who successfully staves off scores of proposals from all manner of feminine fairy, although it could simply be that he prefers the solitary life rather than that he has an actual disdain for the feminine ilk.

Victorian-era Irish writer and folk-lorist David Rice McAnally Jr. amassed an entire volume of Irish legends, *Irish Wonders*, upon which William Butler Yeats and other scholars draw quite heavily. While little is known about McAnally, we do know he was a clergyman who heard many stories including accounts of pookas (you'll find one of my favorites in the chapter on the subject). He wrote one of the best extended descriptions and accompanying stories of the leprechaun to date, which I have excerpted from here.

McAnally describes the leprechaun, or leprechawn, as a creature of neither evil nor good, but of rather mixed quality, the child of an evil father and a degenerate fairy of a mother. (Apparently she spent one too many nights knocking back the whiskey with a pooka.)

The best way to spot a leprechaun is to know what one is looking for. For physical description, McAnally's account is unmatched. He writes:

✳ He is of diminutive size, about three feet high, and is dressed in a little red jacket or round-about, with red breeches buckled at the knee, gray or black stockings, and a hat, cocked in the style of a century ago, over a little, old, withered face. Round his neck is an Elizabethan ruff, and frills of lace are at his wrists. On the wild west coast, where the Atlantic winds bring almost constant rains, he dispenses with ruff and frills and wears a frieze overcoat over his pretty red suit, so that, unless on the lookout for the cocked hat, "ye might pass a Leprechawn on the road and never know it's himself that's in it at all."

In different country districts the Lepre-chawn has different names. In the northern counties he is the Logheryman; in Tipperary, he is the Lurigadawne; in Kerry, the Luricawne; in Monaghan, the Cluricawne. The dress also varies. The Logheryman wears the uniform of some British infantry regiments, a red coat and white breeches, but instead of a cap, he wears a broad-brimmed, high, pointed hat, and after doing some trick more than usually mischievous, his favorite position is to poise himself on the extreme point of his hat, standing at the top of a wall or on a house, feet in the air, then laugh heartily and disappear. The Lurigadawne wears an antique slashed jacket of red, with peaks all round and a jockey cap, also sporting a sword, which he uses as a magic wand. The Luricawne is a fat, pursy little fellow whose jolly round face rivals in redness the cut-a-way jacket he wears, that always has seven rows of seven buttons in each row, though what use they are has never been determined, since his jacket is never buttoned, nor, indeed, can it be, but falls away from a shirt invariably white as the snow. When in full dress he wears a helmet several sizes too large for him, but, in general, prudently discards this article of headgear as having a tendency to render him conspicuous in a country where helmets are obsolete, and wraps his head in a handkerchief that he ties over his ears.

The Cluricawne of Monaghan is a little dandy, being gorgeously arrayed in a swallow-tailed evening coat of red with green vest, white breeches, black stockings, and shoes that "fur the shine av 'em 'ud shame a lookin'-glass." His hat is a long cone without a brim, and is usually set jauntily on one side of his curly head.

When greatly provoked, he will sometimes take vengeance by suddenly ducking and poking the sharp point of his hat into the eye of the offender.

Such conduct is, however, exceptional, as he commonly contents himself with soundly abusing those at whom he has taken offence, the objects of his anger hearing his voice but seeing nothing of his person.

Leprechauns are known to ride goats, sheep, or dogs to get around, and many a peasant has awoken to find their faithful companions muddy and exhausted. In some cases, the leprechaun will ride the animal to its death. Not unlike the mischief-making goblins or brownies, the leprechaun can be blamed for everything from strewn furniture, tumbling babies, and spoilt milk to empty cupboards. By the same hand, the <u>leprechaun is fond of families and becomes quite attached</u>, offering help in the fields and with domestic tasks (as long as he is given his payment of his own fresh food and drink). Do not, under any

When greatly provoked, he will sometimes take vengeance by suddenly ducking and poking the sharp point of his hat into the eye of the offender.

circumstances, attempt to leave the leprechaun or any other domestic fairy a subpar offering of leftovers. They will wreak havoc upon your household, though no one will be permanently harmed.

Their gold, which is possibly stored in brimming pots as part of their greater stash, is more commonly the prize hidden inside a magic purse. Most leprechauns

are in possession of said magic purse, one which never runs dry. It possesses just one shilling, one magical shilling, but there's always another shilling after that, and after that, and after that, and so on.

Curious how to catch one or if it's even possible? In *Irish Wonders*, McAnally offers us three lovely leprechaun encounters. In the first account from a Kerry "peasant," Michael O'Dougherty, "easy money" comes by searching the lands for almost a year, hoping to catch a leprechaun. It also goes without saying that coming back from a wake and napping under a hedge on the way lends a suspicious air of potent beverage consumption to the tale, though this in no way diminishes its strength. (Hey, we've all been there.) Nonetheless, McAnally confirms the idea that any simple distraction will allow the leprechaun to escape. In the second story, the case of Galway's Paddy Donnelly, we hear the

story of a hardworking, sober man who actually manages to get a leprechaun to give up the gold—or so it is believed by all the other townsfolk. For "how else could he get rich at all?" they asked, although Donnelly staunchly denied any leprechaun's involvement in his good fortune. In fact, Donnelly becomes unpopular in the area because he refuses to admit and give up the location of the golden store. The guy just can't win. And finally, the third story tells us about a blaggard (scoundrel) named Dennis O'Bryan of Tipperary. Dennis, who hated hard work and could be found "sitting in a shebeen day in and out" (a shebeen is an unlicensed pub or private house, often looked at with disdain by local pub crawlers), stumbles upon a leprechaun and chokes the little man into submission. Alas, Dennis' grand attempt to avoid hard labor leads him to just that (thirty days, so said the judge).

Michael O'Dougherty & the Leprechaun
by D. R. McAnally

"Mind ye," said a Kerry peasant, "the onliest time ye can ketch the little vagabond is when he's sitting down, an' he never sets down excepting when his brogues want mending. He runs about so much he wears them out, and when he feels his feet on the ground, down he sets under a hedge or behind a wall, or in the grass, and takes them off an' mends them. Then comes you by, as quiet as a cat and sees him there, that ye can easily, be his red coat, an' you slipping up on him, catches him in yer arms.

"'Give up yer gold,' says you.

"'Begob, I've no gold,' says he.

"'Then outs with yer magic purse,' says you.

"But it's like pulling a hat full of teeth to get either purse or gold off him. He's got gold by the ton, and can tell ye where ye can put yer finger on it, but he won't, till ye make him, an' that ye must do be no easy means. Some cuts off his wind be choking him, an' some bates him, but don't for the life o' ye take yer eyes off him, for if ye do, he's off like a flash and the same man never sees him again, and that's how it was with Michael O'Dougherty.

"He was out there looking for nigh a year, for he wanted to get married an' hadn't any money, so he thought the easiest was to catch a Luricawne. So he was looking and watching and the fellers making fun of him all the time.

One night he was coming back from a wake he'd been at, and on the way home he laid under the hedge and slept awhile, thin rose and walked on. So as he was walking, he seen a Luricawne in the grass be the road a-mending his brogues. So he slipped up an' got him fast enough, an' then made him tell him where was his gold. The Luricawne took him to nigh the place in the break o' the hills an' was going for to show him, when all at once Mike heard the most uproarious screech over the head of him that would make the hairs of ye head stand up like a mad cat's tail.

"'The saints defend me,' says he, 'what's that?' And he looked up from the Luricawne that he was carrying in his arms. That minute the little man went out of his sight, for he looked away from it and it was gone, but he heard it laugh when it went and he never got the gold but died poor, as me father knows, and he a boy when it happened."

Paddy Donnelly's Get-Rich Scheme

by D. R. McAnally

"Paddy Donnelly of Connemara was always hard at work as far as any could see, and bad luck to the day he'd miss, barring Sundays. When all would go to the

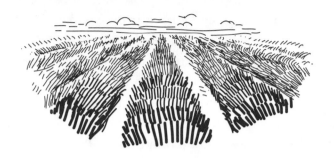

fair, not a foot he'd stir to go near it, no more did a drop of drink cross his lips. When they'd ask him why he didn't take diversion, he'd laugh and tell them his field was diversion enough for him, and by and by he got rich, so they knew that when they were at the fair or wakes or sports, it was looking for a Leprechawn he was and not working, and he got one too, for how else could he get rich at all?"

And so it must have been, in spite of the denials of Paddy Donnelly, though, to do him justice, he stoutly affirmed that his small property was acquired by industry, economy, and temperance. But according to the opinions of his neighbors, "bad scran to him, twas as greedy as a pig he was, for he knew where the gold was, and wanted it all for himself, and so lied about it like the Leprechawns, that's known to be the biggest liars in the world."

Dennis O'Bryan & The Magic Purse

by D. R. McAnally

"Now Dennis was a young blaggard that was always after peeping about under the hedge for to catch a Leprechawn, though they do say that them that doesn't search after them sees them oftener than them that does, but Dennis made his mind up that if there was one in the country, he'd have him, for he hated work worse than sin, and did be sitting in a shebeen day in and out till you'd think he'd grow on the seat. So one day he was coming home, and he seen something red over in the corner o' the field, and in he goes, as quiet as a mouse, and up on the Leprechawn and grips him be the collar and down's him on the ground.

"'Arrah, now, ye ugly little vagabond,' says he, 'I've got ye at last. Now give up yer gold, or by Jakers I'll

choke the life out of yer pin-squeezing corkage, ye old cobbler, ye,' says he, shaking him fit to make his head drop off.

"The Leprechawn begged, and screeched, and cried, and said he wasn't a real Leprechawn that was in it, but a young one that hadn't any gold, but Dennis wouldn't let go of him, and at last the Leprechawn said he'd take him to the pot of gold that was hid by the say, in a glen in Clare. Dennis didn't want to go so far, being afeared the Leprechawn would get away, and he thought the devilish bastard was after lying to him, because he known there was gold closer than that, and so he was choking him that his eyes stood out till ye could knock 'em off with a stick, and the Leprechawn asked him would he leave go if he'd give him the magic purse. Dennis thought he'd better do it, for he was mortally afeared the audacious little villain would do him some trick and get away, so he took the purse, after looking at it to make sure it was red silk, and had the shilling in it, but the minute he took his two eyes off the Leprechawn, away went the rogue with a laugh that Dennis didn't like at all.

"But he was feeling very comfortable, by reason of getting the purse, and says to himself, 'Begorra, 'tis meself that'll ate the full of me waistband for one time, and drink till a steam engine can't squeeze one more drop more down me neck,' says he, and off he goes like a quarter-horse for Miss Clooney's shebeen, that's where he used for to go. In he goes, and there was Paddy Grogan, and Tim O'Donovan, and Mike Conathey, and Bryan Flaherty, and a string more of them sitting on the table, and he pulls up a seat and down he sets, a-callin' to Miss Clooney to bring her best.

"'Where's yer money?' says she to him, for he didn't use to have none barring a tuppence or so.

"'Do you have no fear,' says he, 'for the money,' says he, 'ye penny-scrapin' old skeleton,' this was beways of a shot at her, for it was the size of a load o' hay she was, and weighed a ton. 'Do you bring yer best,' says he. 'I'm a gentleman of fortune, bad luck to the job o' work I'll do till the life leaves me. Come, gentlemen, drink at my expense.' And so they did and more than once, and after four or five guns apiece, Dennis ordered dinner for them all, but Miss Clooney told him sore the bit or not one sip more would cross the lips of him till he paid for that he had. So out he pulls the magic purse for to pay, and to show it them and told them what it was and where he got it.

"'And was it the Leprechawn give it ye?' says they.

"'It was,' says Dennis, 'and the virtue of this purse is such, that if ye take shillins out of it be the handful all day long, they'll be coming in a stream like whiskey out of a jug,' says he, pulling out one.

"And thin, me jewel, he put in his fingers after another, but it wasn't there, for the Leprechawn made a ijit of him, and instead of giving him the right purse, gave him one just like it, so as unless ye looked close, ye couldn't make out the difference between them. But the face on Dennis was a holy show when he seen the Leprechawn had done him, and he with only a shilling, an' half a crown of drink down the throats of them.

"'To the devil with you and yer Leprechawns, and purses, and magic shillins,' screamed Miss Clooney, believing, and small blame to her that's, that it was lying to her he was. 'Ye're a thief, so ye are, drinking up me drink, with a lie on yer lips about the purse, and insulting me into the bargain,' says she, thinking how he called her a skeleton, and her a load for a wagging. 'Yer impudence beats old Nick, so it does,' says she; so she up and hits him a power of a crack on the head with a bottle; and the other fellys, a-thinking sure that it was a lie he was after telling them, and he leaving them to pay for the drink he'd had, got on him and belted him out of the face till it was nigh onto dead he was. Then a constable comes along and hears the phillaloo they did be making and comes in.

"'Tatter and agers,' says he, 'leave off. I command the peace. What's the matter here?'

"So they told him and he agreed that Dennis stole the purse and took him be the collar.

"'Leave go,' says Dennis. 'Sure what's the harm o' getting the purse of a Leprechawn?'

"'None at all,' says the policeman, 'if ye produce the Leprechawn and make him testify he gave it ye and that ye haven't been burglarious and circumvented another man's money,' says he.

"But Dennis couldn't do it, so the constable tumbled him into the jail. From that he went to court and got

thirty days at hard labor, that he never done in his life afore, an' after he got out, he said he'd left lookin' for Leprechawns, for they were too smart for him entirely, an' it's true for him, because I believe they were."

> *If you stepped out of the shower and saw a leprechaun standing at the base of your toilet, would you scream, or would you innately understand that he meant you no harm?*
>
> DAVID SEDARIS, **FROM** LET'S EXPLORE
> DIABETES WITH OWLS

Fairies You'll Fall For: Tree Spirits

The association with spirits of the trees and tree enchantments is at the core of fairy belief around the world. In Northern Sweden you will find a *Vittra* or *Vaettr*, a nature spirit, under which elves and dwarves fall. In Japan the forests are full of *Tengu*, winged fairies who can shapeshift into other beings, especially animals. The *Lunantishees* guard the blackthorn trees and will bring great misfortune upon you should you be foolish enough to cut from the tree on either November 11 or May 11. Of course the Celts as well as the Druids held trees in such high regard that there is no denying this influence today on the fairy faith. <u>Oak trees were sacred to druids along with mistletoe</u>, giving way to our traditions today of decking our halls with mistletoe at the holidays. (No word yet on whether or not the Druids made out underneath it.) Cassandra Eason, in her *A Complete Guide to Fairies and Magical Beings*, reminds us that *Hyldermoder*, or Elder Mothers, live in elder trees. They are harmless, unless of course you try to harm the tree.

Many origin stories of dryads or forest nymphs tell stories not unlike the story that follows here: that the entities within the tree were actually once human, transformed by the supernatural powers of a witch or other powerful magical being. It should be noted that the witchy powers are rarely wielded willy-nilly, as many a modern story may indicate. Consider that fairy tales are invented and reinvented, passed down through oral history and tradition, and are quite subject to the fads of the societal times. So the wicked witch, who strikes just to be mean or just because she is evil, became more common in tales during and after the seventeenth century's infamous witch craze. The "poor prince" in our next story makes the mistake of trying to strike a witch's wolf (let that be a warning to all of you).

Still, in order to turn a mortal man into a beast or transform him into a comatose or trapped state, as the witch does here by "freezing" the prince into the elm tree, something usually takes place to "zap" the human.

In the Snow White story, the witch offers the poison apple that sends our heroine into a deep sleep. Sometimes, inhalation of (ahem) smoke will be the catalyst. Water is the most common form of mistaken ingestion. The weary traveler seeks to quench their thirst. Alas, such is the case with the foolish prince in the next tale. He drank the cursed Kool-Aid of sorts.

Henry Beston was an American writer and naturalist born in Boston. After his stint as an ambulance driver in World War I ended, he returned to the US shaken. He retreated to Cape Cod, where he spent an entire year immersed in life on the beach, observing nature and writing. His best-known work, *The Outermost House*, is a literary classic that is also credited as helping establish the Cape Cod National Seashore. Rachel Carson even once said that Henry Beston was the only writer who ever influenced her own writing, and Beston is considered one of the fathers of the American environmental movement. Prior to writing *The Outermost House*, which was published in 1928, Beston—whilst communing with nature and seeking the solitude of the woods and wilds—wrote *The Firelight Fairy Book*, first published in 1919. Beston was pals with President Theodore Roosevelt's son, Col. Theodore Roosevelt, and the 1922 edition includes a preface from the younger

Teddy, eschewing the dreary label of "grown-up." The following story is from that collection.

Surely Beston was aware of the sacred beliefs in the elm and the forest spirits of old lore. Anyone who spends so much time in the forest becomes acquainted with the tiny noises and particular smells that lead to confusion and enchantment and lead one ultimately to ponder the magic of it all. You will find many references to the Fairy Kingdom in Beston's story, though they appear under different names from what you may know. Who would not want to watch as The King of the Trees comes into the haunted wood on Midsummer Eve? Midsummer Eve, of course, is a time long believed

to be the night when fairies cavort in the open (à la *A Midsummer Night's Dream*) and magic is afoot. Note also the reference to the mythical British king and enchanter, Gorbodoc, pal to the King of Trees, and remember that Beston was harkening back to a time when the king of Britain was an enchanter and held many powers that we might deem supernatural today. Join Beston as he romps through the love story of a foolish prince, an enchanted tree, and the young maiden activist who sought to save them both.

The Enchanted Elm

by Henry Beston

Once upon a time, while riding, a brave, young prince dashed merrily ahead of his friends, and after galloping across a ploughed field, turned his horse's head down a grassy road leading to a wood. For some time he cantered easily along, expecting any moment to hear the shouts and halloos of his friends following after; but they by mistake took quite another road, and no sound except the pounding of his courser's hoofs reached the Prince's ear. Suddenly an ugly snarl and a short bark broke the stillness of the pleasant forest, and looking down, the Prince saw a gray wolf snapping at his horse's heels.

Though the horse, wild with fear, threatened to run away any instant, the Prince leaned over and struck the wolf with his whip.

Hardly had he done so, when an angry voice cried, "How dare you strike my pet?"

A little distance ahead, a wicked old witch stood at one side of the road. With its tail between its legs, the wolf cowered close to her skirts, and showed its long yellow fangs.

"Pet, indeed!" cried the Prince. "Keep him away from my horse or I will strike him again."

"At your peril, Prince," answered the witch. And then, as the Prince turned his horse's head and gal-

loped back, she called out, "You shall rue this day! You shall rue this day!"

Now by the time the Prince had arrived at the ploughed field and the great road again, his friends had galloped on so far that they were lost to sight. Thinking that he might overtake them by following a shorter road, he turned down a byway skirting the wood in which he had encountered the enchantress. Presently he began to feel very thirsty. Chancing to see an old peasant woman in the fields, the Prince called to her and asked where he could find a roadside spring.

Now this old peasant woman was the wicked witch under another form. Overjoyed at having the Prince fall so easily into her power, she curtsied; and replied that within the wood was to be found the finest spring in the country. Anxious not to lose time, the Prince begged her to lead him to the water. Little did he know that the witch was leading him back into the wood, and that she had just bewitched the water!

When they arrived at the pool, the Prince dismounted, and kneeling by the brim, made a cup of his hands and drank till his thirst was satisfied.

He was just about to seize his horse again by the bridle and put his foot into the stirrup, when a terrible pang shot through his body, darkness swam before

He was just about to seize his horse again by the bridle and put his foot into the stirrup, when a terrible pang shot through his body, darkness swam before his eyes, his arms lengthened and became branches, his fingers, twigs; his feet shot into the ground, and he found himself turned into a giant elm.

his eyes, his arms lengthened and became branches, his fingers, twigs; his feet shot into the ground, and he found himself turned into a giant elm.

A giant elm he was; a giant elm he remained. Unable to find him after a long search, his friends gave him up for lost, and a new Prince ruled over the land. Though the elm tried many times to tell passers-by of his plight, none ever seemed to understand his words. Again and again, when simple wood-cutters ventured into the great dark wood, he would tell them his story and cry out, "I am the Prince! I am the Prince!" But the wood-cutters heard only the wind stirring in the branches. Ah, how cold it was in winter when the skies were steely black and the giant stars sparkled icily! And how pleasant it was when spring returned, and the gossipy birds came back again!

The first year a pair of wood-pigeons took to house-keeping in his topmost branches. The Prince was glad to welcome them, for though denied human speech, he understood the language of trees and birds. On Midsummer Eve, the pigeons said to him, "To-night the King of the Trees comes through the wood. Do you not hear the stir in the forest? All the real trees are pre-paring for the King's coming; they are shedding dead leaves and shaking out their branches."

"Tell me of the King," said the Prince.

"He is tall and dark and strong," said the doves. "He dwells in a great pine in the North. On Midsummer Eve, he goes through the world to see if all is well with the tree people."

"Do you think he can help me?" asked the Prince.

"You might ask him," replied the doves.

The long, long twilight of Midsummer Eve came to a close; night folded the world beneath its starry curtains. At twelve o'clock, though not a breath of air was stirring, the trees were shaken as if by a mighty wind, the rustling of the leaves blending into strange and lovely music, and presently the King of the Trees entered the haunted wood. Even as the wood-doves had said, he was tall and dark and stately.

"Is all well with you, O my people?" said the King, in a voice as sweet and solemn as the wind in the branches on a summer's day.

"Yes, all is well," answered the trees softly. Though some replied, "I have lost a branch," and a little tree called out unhappily, "My neighbors are shutting out all my sunlight."

"Then fare ye well, my people, till next Midsummer Eve," said the stately King. And he was about to stride

onward through the dark wood when the enchanted Prince called aloud to him!

"Stay, O King of the Trees," cried the poor Prince. "Hear me even though I am not of your people. I am a mortal, a prince, and a wicked witch has turned me into a tree. Can you not help me?"

"Alas, poor friend, I can do nothing," replied the King. "However, do not despair. In my travels through the world, I shall surely find someone who can help you. Look for me on next Midsummer Eve."

So the great elm swayed his branches sadly, and the King went on his way.

The winter came again, silent and dark and cold. At the return of spring, a maiden who dwelt with a family of wood-cutters came often to rest in the shade of the great tree. Her father had once been a rich merchant, but evil times had overtaken him, and at his death the only relatives who could be found to take care of the little girl were a family of rough wood-cutters in the royal service. These grudging folk kept the poor maiden always hard at work and gave her the most difficult household tasks. The Prince, who knew the whole story, pitied her very much, and ended by falling quite in love with her. As for the unhappy maiden, it seemed to her that beneath the sheltering shade of the great elm she enjoyed a peace and happiness to be found nowhere else.

Now it was the custom of the wood-men to cut down, during the summer, such trees as would be needed for the coming winter, and one day the woodcutter in whose family the maiden dwelt announced his intention of cutting down the great elm.

"Not the great elm which towers above all the forest?" cried the maiden.

"Yes, that very tree," answered the woodcutter gruffly. "To-morrow morning we shall fell it to the ground, and to-morrow night we shall build the midsummer fire with its smaller branches. What are you crying about, you silly girl?"

"Oh, please don't cut the great elm!" begged the good maiden.

"Nonsense!" said the woodcutter. "I wager you have been wasting your time under its branches. I shall certainly cut the tree down in the morning."

All night long, you may be sure, the maiden pondered on

the best way to save the great tree; and since she was as clever as she was good, she at length hit upon a plan. Rising early on Midsummer Morn, she ran to the forest, climbed the great elm, and concealed herself in its topmost branches. She saw the rest of the wood beneath her, and the distant peaks of the Adamant Mountains; and she rejoiced in the dawn songs of the birds.

An hour after the sun had risen, she heard the voices of the wood-cutter and his men as they came through the wood. Soon the band arrived at the foot of the tree. Imagine the feelings of the poor Prince when he saw the sharp axes at hand to cut him down!

"I shall strike the first blow," said the chief wood-cutter, and he lifted his axe in the air.

Suddenly from the tree-top a warning voice sang,

"Throw the axe down, harm not me.
I am an enchanted tree.
He who strikes shall breathe his last,
Before Midsummer Eve hath passed."

"There is a spirit in the tree," cried the woodcutters, thoroughly frightened. "Let us hurry away from here before it does us a mischief." And in spite of all the chief wood-cutter's remonstrances, they ran away as fast as their legs could carry them.

The chief wood-cutter, however, was bolder-hearted, and lifted the axe again. As the blade shone uplifted in the sun, the maiden sang once more,

"Throw the axe down, harm not me.
I am an enchanted tree.
He who strikes shall breathe his last
Before Midsummer Eve hath passed."

Hearing the voice again, the chief began to feel just the littlest bit alarmed; nevertheless, he stood his ground and lifted the axe a third time. Once more the girl sang,

*"Throw the axe down, harm not me.
I am an enchanted tree.
He who strikes shall breathe his last
Before Midsummer Eve hath passed."*

At the same moment, the elm managed to throw down a great branch which struck the rogue a sound thump on the shoulders. Now thoroughly terrified, the chief wood-cutter himself fled from the spot.

All day long, for fear lest he return, the maiden remained hidden in the tree. At twilight, overcome by weariness, she fell into a deep sleep. Just before midnight, alas, she was awakened from her slumber by hearing an angry voice cry, "Come down from the tree, wicked, deceitful girl, or I shall cut it down at once!"

Very much alarmed, the poor maiden looked down through the branches, and discovered the wood-cutter standing at the foot of the elm. A lantern swung from his left hand, and his sharpest axe rested on his right shoulder. He had returned home, and not finding the maiden there, had suspected that it was her voice which had frightened his men away.

"Come down," roared the rascal. "I'll teach you, you minx, to play tricks with me.

One—two—three." And lifting the axe in the air, he was about to send it crashing into the trunk of the elm, when the mysterious murmur which heralded the coming of the King of the Trees sounded through the wood. Perplexed and frightened again, the chief wood-cutter let fall his axe. Presently he perceived two beings coming toward him through the solemn forest. Uttering a howl of fear, the rogue would have fled, but, lifting his wand, the elder of the newcomers transfixed him to the spot. The two personages were the King of the Trees and his friend, the mighty enchanter, Gorbodoc.

"Descend and fear not, maiden," said the King of the Trees. "You have done bravely and well. Your misfortunes are over, and a happier day is at hand."

So the brave girl hurried down the tree, and stood before the enchanter and the King. Very pretty she was, too, in her rustic dress and ribbons.

Lifting his wand with great solemnity, Gorbodoc touched the trunk of the elm. There was a blinding flash of rosy fire; the great tree appeared to shrink and dissolve, and presently the Prince stood before them.

"Welcome, Prince," said the enchanter.

"Your enemy, the witch, will trouble you no more. I have turned her into an owl and given her to the Queen of Lantern Land. As for you," and here the enchanter turned fiercely upon the wood-cutter, "you shall be a green monkey, until you have planted and brought to full growth as many trees as you have cut down."

An instant later, a green monkey swung off into the tree-tops.

Then the grateful Prince thanked the King of the Trees, the mighty Gorbodoc, and the brave maiden, with all his heart. I am glad to say that he got his castle back again and married the maiden who had saved his life, and they lived happily ever after.

Flower Fables

The summer moon shone brightly down upon the sleeping earth, while far away from mortal eyes danced the Fairy folk. Fire-flies hung in bright clusters on the dewy leaves, that waved in the cool night-wind; and the flowers stood gazing, in very wonder, at the little Elves, who lay among the fern-leaves, swung in the vine-boughs, sailed on the lake in lily cups, or danced on the mossy ground, to the music of the hare-bells, who rung out their merriest peal in honor of the night. Under the shade of a wild rose sat the Queen and her little Maids of Honor, beside the silvery mushroom where the feast was spread.

"Now, my friends," said she, "to while away the time till the bright moon goes down, let us each tell a tale, or relate what we have done or learned this day. I will begin with you, Sunny Lock," added she, turning to a lovely little Elf, who lay among the fragrant leaves of a primrose.

With a gay smile, "Sunny Lock" began her story.

"As I was painting the bright petals of a blue bell, it told me this tale."

Louisa May Alcott

The Brownie

———◦◦———

With little debate, the most adored among the fairy kin is the brownie and his counterparts. Referred to on occasion as a house pixie or elf and sometimes an imp, the brownie is a dedicated creature who likes hard work and a clean house. He does not take payment for his work, but will take a good piece of cake and a dish of milk each night. Some like to have water for a bath. In addition, one must match the brownie's standards for a clean home. If you are lazy you will wake up to find you've been pinched black and blue by the brownie in the night (they do have a mischievous side).

He is called *Stoechia* in Greece, *Duende* in Spain, *Para* in Finland. It is said the Finnish version stole milk from the neighbor's cows, just a little from each one, until the household had an abundance. On more than one occasion a brownie has turned against the homeowners when wronged or left in squalor. The results are hardly noticeable in a messy house, but eventually you will find yourself missing very significant items. This is the brownie at work. In parts of Scandinavia, the *Niss* or *Nisse* is a similar creature who assigns himself to a family or farm. In Scotland, you will also find the *Dobbie* or *Dobie* (fans of J. K. Rowling will recognize this guy as Dobby), a helpful creature, although slightly more dim-witted than the clever brownie. Imps tend to have

many of the same qualities of the goblins, brownies, and house-elves but with a decidedly more devilish quality, and are widely considered the most clever of any fairy creature.

Louise Imogen Guiney was born in Boston in 1861 and, after a good education and stints as a postal worker and librarian, moved to Oxford, England, in 1901. She was a poet and essay writer, who gave up poetry due to ill health (she died of a stroke in 1920) and began to concentrate on collections of works by English poets and writers, including Robert Louis Stevenson. From her work *Brownies and Bogles* we find the following excerpt on the subject:

> The English names for the affable Brownie-folk bring to our minds the most wayward, frolicsome elves of all fairydom. Boggart was the Yorkshire sprite, and the Boggart commonly disliked children, and stole their food and playthings; wherein he differed from his kindly kindred. Hobgoblin (Hop-goblin) was so called because he hopped on one leg. Hobgoblin is the same as Rob or Bob-Goblin, a goblin whose full name seemed to be Robert. Robin Hood, the famous outlaw, dear to all of us, was thought to have been christened after Robin

Hood the fairy, because he, too, was tricksy and sportive, wore a hood, and lived in the deep forest.

In Ireland lived the mocking, whimsical little Fir-Darrig, Robin Goodfellow's own twin. He dressed in tight-fitting red; Fir-Darrig itself meant "the red man." He had big humorous ears, and the softest and most flexible voice in the world, which could mimic any sound at will. He sat by the fire, and smoked a pipe, big as himself, belonging to the man of the house. He loved cleanliness, brought good-luck to his abode, and, like a cat, generally preferred places to people.

Brownies tend to be around knee height or smaller, although their height, just as their temperament, varies. They do not value gold or money in any way but, in addition to cakes and cream, never refuse a payment of fine material or tiny clothing. They love silks and velvet and love to dress well in spite of their domestic occupation. In Germany, they are called *Kobolds* but are frequently seen as naked little beings. They tend to attach themselves to tailors, seamstresses, and even milliners, doing endless scrubbing in exchange for yards of silk.

Ol' brownie o' the glen
Had no fear of men
But should you leave no wine
Men'd be fearin' offa him.

—DIEDRE O'ROURKE, FROM "WHICH WAY
THE WILL O' THE WISP"

Sometimes you will find brownies in grand hotels or bed and breakfasts, where they prove themselves most useful. However, they do have a tendency to take things that have been left behind, so mind your watch if a brownie is suspected on site. All in all they tend to be merry creatures who have managed to coexist happily with mortals for hundreds of years, if not longer. In the following story from Elizabeth W. Grierson's collection, *The Scottish Fairy Book*, we see the brownie as hero.

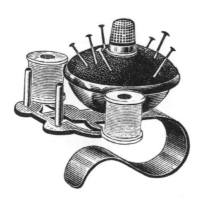

The Brownie O' Ferne-Den

by Elizabeth W. Grierson

There have been many Brownies known in Scotland; and stories have been written about the Brownie o' Bodsbeck and the Brownie o' Blednock, but about neither of them has a prettier story been told than that which I am going to tell you about the Brownie o' Ferne-Den.

Now, Ferne-Den was a farmhouse, which got its name from the glen, or "den," on the edge of which it stood, and through which anyone who wished to reach the dwelling had to pass.

And this glen was believed to be the abode of a Brownie, who never appeared to anyone in the daytime, but who, it was said, was sometimes seen at night, stealing about, like an ungainly shadow, from tree to tree, trying to keep from observation, and never, by any chance, harming anybody.

Indeed, like all Brownies that are properly treated and let alone, so far was he from harm-

Indeed, like all Brownies that are properly treated and let alone, so far was he from harming anybody that he was always on the lookout to do a good turn to those who needed his assistance.

ing anybody that he was always on the look-out to do a good turn to those who needed his assistance.

The farmer often said that he did not know what he would do without him; for if there was any work to be finished in a hurry at the farm—corn to thrash, or winnow, or tie up into bags, turnips to cut, clothes to wash, a kirn to be kirned, a garden to be weeded—all that the farmer and his wife had to do was to leave the door of the barn, or the turnip shed, or the milk house open when they went to bed, and put down a bowl of new milk on the doorstep for the Brownie's supper, and when they woke the next morning the bowl would be empty, and the job finished better than if it had been done by mortal hands.

In spite of all this, however, which might have proved to them how gentle and kindly the Creature really was, everyone about the place was afraid of him, and would rather go a couple of miles round about in the dark, when they were coming home from Kirk or Market, than pass through the glen, and run the risk of catching a glimpse of him.

I said that they were all afraid of him, but that was not true, for the farmer's wife was so good and gentle that she was not afraid of anything, and when the Brownie's supper had to be left outside, she always filled his bowl with the richest milk, and added a good spoonful of cream to it, for, said she, "He works so hard for us, and asks no wages, he well deserves the very best meal that we can give him."

One night this gentle lady was taken very ill, and everyone was afraid that she was going to die. Of course, her husband was greatly distressed, and so were her servants, for she had been such a good Mistress to them that they loved her as if she had been their mother. But they were all young, and none of them knew very much about illness, and everyone agreed that it would be better to send off for an old woman who lived about seven miles away on the other side of the river, who was known to be a very skilful nurse.

But who was to go? That was the question. For it was black midnight, and the way to the old woman's house lay straight through the glen. And whoever travelled that road ran the risk of meeting the dreaded Brownie.

The farmer would have gone only too willingly, but he dare not leave his wife alone; and the servants stood in groups about the kitchen, each one telling the other that he ought to go, yet no one offering to go themselves.

Little did they think that the cause of all their terror, a queer, wee, misshapen little man, all covered with hair, with a long beard, red-rimmed eyes, broad, flat feet, just like the feet of a paddock, and enormous long arms that touched the ground, even when he stood upright, was within a yard or two of them, listening to their talk, with an anxious face, behind the kitchen door.

For he had come up as usual, from his hiding-place in the glen, to see if there were any work for him to do, and to look for his bowl of milk. And he had seen, from the open door and lit-up windows, that there was something wrong inside the farmhouse, which at that hour was wont to be dark, and still, and silent; and he had crept into the entry to try and find out what the matter was.

When he gathered from the servants' talk that the Mistress, whom he loved so dearly, and who had been so kind to him, was ill, his heart sank within him; and when he heard that the silly servants were so taken up with their own fears that they dared not set out to fetch a nurse for her, his contempt and anger knew no bounds.

"Fools, idiots, dolts!" he muttered to himself, stamping his queer, misshapen feet on the floor. "They speak as if a body were ready to take a bite off them as soon as ever he met them. If they only knew the bother it gives me to keep out of their road they wouldna be so silly. But, by my troth, if they go on like this, the bonnie lady will die amongst their fingers. So it strikes me that Brownie must e'en gang himself."

So saying, he reached up his hand, and took down a dark cloak which belonged to the farmer, which was hanging on a peg on the wall, and, throwing it over his head and shoulders, or as somewhat to hide his ungainly form, he hurried away to the stable, and saddled and bridled the fleetest-footed horse that stood there.

When the last buckle was fastened, he led it to the door and scrambled on its back. "Now, if ever thou travelledst fleetly, travel fleetly now," he said; and it was as if the creature understood him, for it gave a little whinny and pricked up its ears; then it darted out into the darkness like an arrow from the bow.

In less time than the distance had ever been ridden in before, the Brownie drew rein at the old woman's cottage.

She was in bed, fast asleep; but he rapped sharply on the window, and when she rose and put her old face, framed in its white mutch, close to the pane to ask who was there, he bent forward and told her his errand.

"Thou must come with me, Goodwife, and that quickly," he commanded, in his deep, harsh voice, "if the Lady of Ferne-Den's life is to be saved; for there is no one to nurse her up-bye at the farm there, save a lot of empty-headed servant wenches."

"But how am I to get there? Have they sent a cart for me?" asked the old woman anxiously; for, as far as she could see, there was nothing at the door save a horse and its rider.

"No, they have sent no cart," replied the Brownie, shortly. "So you must just climb up behind me on the saddle, and hang on tight to my waist, and I'll promise to land ye at Ferne-Den safe and sound."

His voice was so masterful that the old woman dare not refuse to do as she was bid; besides, she had often ridden pillion-wise when she was a lassie, so she made haste to dress herself, and when she was ready she unlocked her door, and, mounting the louping-on stane that stood beside it, she was soon seated behind the dark-cloaked stranger, with her arms clasped tightly round him.

Not a word was spoken till they approached the dreaded glen, then the old woman felt her cour-

age giving way. "Do ye think that there will be any chance of meeting the Brownie?" she asked timidly. "I would fain not run the risk, for folk say that he is an unchancy creature."

Her companion gave a curious laugh. "Keep up your heart, and dinna talk havers," he said, "for I promise ye ye'll see naught uglier this night than the man whom ye ride behind."

"Oh, then, I'm fine and safe," replied the old woman, with a sigh of relief, "for although I havena' seen your face, I warrant that ye are a true man, for the care you have taken of a poor old woman."

She relapsed into silence again till the glen was passed and the good horse had turned into the farmyard. Then the horseman slid to the ground, and, turning round, lifted her carefully down in his long, strong arms. As he did so the cloak slipped off him, revealing his short, broad body and his misshapen limbs.

"In a' the world, what kind o' man are ye?" she asked, peering into his face in the grey morning light, which was just dawning. "What makes your eyes so big? And what have ye done to your feet? They are more like paddock's webs than aught else."

The queer little man laughed again. "I've wandered many a mile in my time without a horse to help me, and I've heard it said that ower much walking makes the feet unshapely," he replied. "But waste no time in talking, good Dame. Go thy way into the house; and, hark'ee, if anyone asks thee who brought thee hither so quickly, tell them that there was a lack of men, so thou hadst e'en to be content to ride behind the Brownie O' Ferne-Den."

> *O'er hill, o'er dale, through*
> *   bush, through briar,*
> *O'er parke, o'er pale, through*
> *   flood, through fire,*
> *I do wander everie where, swifter*
> *   then y Moons sphere;*
> *And I serve the Fairy Queene, to dew*
> *   her orbs upon the green.*
>
> WILLIAM SHAKESPEARE,
> *A MIDSUMMER NIGHT'S DREAM*

Goblins, Coblyns, and Dwarves

There is some discussion on the nature of goblins and whether they should be feared or fancied. William Wirt Sikes, in his Victorian-era tome of Welsh folklore, *British*

Goblins, believes the word goblin refers to a coblyn—a cave or mine-dwelling fairy characterized by knocking. While their knocking can help identify pockets of gems or other precious metals, a distinct three-knock sound can predict misfortune or even death.

The coblyn is somewhat akin to the dwarf. Just as we know of seven very industrious dwarves with hearts of gold, we see throughout folktales that dwarves and other mine-dwelling fairies seek to help those who work industriously beside them. Dwarves are often portrayed as cheerful and friendly, although over time they have become more isolated and prefer the company of each other and the solitary miner. (It is interesting to note that a coblyn and the term cobbler may have some overlap, especially because the knocking of the cobbler's tools upon the bench is not unlike the knocking of the mine.)

Thomas Keightley tells this story of a band of dwarves in Germany, which shows the classic "one bad apple" syndrome and how it has led to the isolation of the dwarf population in general:

> A baker, who lived in the valley between Blenkenburg and Quedlinburg, used to remark that a part of the loaves he

baked was always missing, though he never could find out the thief. This continual secret theft was gradually reducing him to poverty. At last he began to suspect the Dwarfs of being the cause of his misfortune. He accordingly got a bunch of little twigs, and beating the air with them in all directions, at length struck the mist-caps off some Dwarfs, who could now conceal themselves no longer. There was a great noise made about it; several other Dwarfs were caught in the act of committing theft, and at last the whole of the Dwarf-people were forced to quit the country. In order, in some degree, to indemnify the inhabitants for what had been stolen, and at the same time to be able to estimate the number of those that departed, a large cask was set up on what is now called Kirch-berg, near the village of Thele, into which each Dwarf was to cast a piece of money. This cask was found, after the departure of the Dwarfs, to be quite filled with ancient coins, so great was their number.

The Dwarf-people went by Warnstadt, a village not far from Quedlinburg, still going toward the east. Since that time the Dwarfs have disappeared out of this country; and it is only now and then that a solitary one may be seen.

In Germany we also find the *Wichtlein*, little old men with long beards who haunt the mines to the south. Some called them *Haus-schmiedlein* or *House-smiths*, for the sound of the anvil that is associated with them. Kobolds are also found in mines in Germany, mostly making trouble and stealing tools.

And, of course, we mustn't forget the *Tommyknocker*, a magical class of fairies who haunt mines throughout England, Cornwall, and parts of North America—no

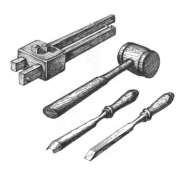

doubt brought over with the Cornish miners in the 1800s. They are said to be helpful and can aid in the business of finding gold and gemstones and the like, but are quick to take offense and are often blamed for mining accidents.

Some believe tommyknockers to be the spirits of those who died in cave-ins and other such tragedies.

In *Cornish Legends*, Robert Hunt describes fairy miners as the Knockers:

> At Ransom Mine the "Knockers" were always very active in their sub-terranean operations. In every part of the mine their "knockings" were heard, but most especially were they busy in one particular "end." The story continues to describe an old man and his

Some believe tommyknockers to be the spirits of those who died in cave-ins and other such tragedies.

son who could communicate with the Knockers, and on a Midsummer's Eve learned the secret to where the greatest "lode" was in the mine. For every amount of wealth he took, he must leave 1/10th for the Knockers. The old man complied and became very wealthy along with his son. When the old man died, the son grew greedy and tried to cheat the Knockers by not leaving the share. His lode failed and he died a penniless beggar.

Other mountain-dwelling fairies include the *Gwyllion*, related to the Welsh ellyllon. Where as ellylon are elves that live in forests and glens, the gwyllion roam lonely roads in the mountains. The Welsh word *gwyll* can be used to mean gloom, shade, duskiness, a fairy, a hag, or a goblin, but especially these particular female fairies who lurk in the high hills.

Similar to a hobgoblin or brownie, the domestic *Bwbach* or *Boobach* is a Welsh goblin who helps around the house. Like the brownie, the goblin requires a certain payment (in advance) for services rendered. Sikes writes:

The maid having swept the kitchen, makes a good fire the last thing at night, and having put the churn, filled with cream, on the whitened hearth, with a basin of fresh cream for the Bwbach on the hob, goes to bed to await the event. In the morning she finds (if she is in luck) that the Bwbach has emptied the basin of cream, and plied the churn-dasher so well that the maid has but to give a thump or two to bring the butter in a great lump. Like the Ellyll which it so much resembles, the Bwbach does not approve of dissenters and their ways, and especially strong is its aversion to total abstainers.

In France, goblins are called *Gobelin* or *Lutin* or sometimes *Follet*, and throw stones when angered. They are very fond of children and horses, though they were known to tease the former, though never the latter.

The following story, however, from Yei Theodora Ozaki's 1908 collection, *Japanese Fairy Tales*, takes rather a different view of the goblin. Ozaki writes that the idea for the compilation of folk tales came at the suggestion of Andrew Lang of Fairy Book fame (*The Red Fairy Book*, *The Yellow Fairy Book*, etc.). Born in 1872, Yei Theodora

Ozaki was a fearless woman in her own right. A collector and translator of Japanese folklore, a world traveler, and a woman of fierce independent spirit, she was born to Baron Ozaki and Catharine Morrison. Her parents divorced after five years and Yei spent time living both with her mother in Europe as well as in Japan with her father. When her father attempted to arrange a marriage for her, she refused and instead set out for adventure. She traveled all around the world, working as a secretary and a teacher to pay her way, and gathering stories wherever she went.

This is a cautionary tale: should you find yourself alone in the woods with nowhere to turn but a ramshackle cottage, and should you peek into a room you are warned not to, you better be prepared to run. Fast.

Yei lived an adventure-filled and exciting life, translating many traditional Japanese fairy tales to an English-speaking audience. Her collections remain seminal, as the Brothers Grimm of the Far East.

This is a cautionary tale: should you find yourself alone in the woods with nowhere to turn but a ramshackle cottage, and should you peek into a room you are warned not to, you better be prepared to run. Fast.

If that doesn't work, call on Buddha to save you because when you meet the Cannibal Goblin, your choices are few and your chances are slim. You've been warned.

The Goblin of Adachigahara

by Yei Theodora Ozaki

Long, long ago there was a large plain called Adachigahara, in the province of Mutsu in Japan. This place was said to be haunted by a cannibal goblin who took the form of an old woman. From time to time many travelers disappeared and were never heard of more, and the old women round the charcoal braziers in the evenings, and the girls washing the household rice at the wells in the mornings, whispered dreadful stories of how the missing folk had been lured to the goblin's cottage and devoured, for the goblin lived only on human flesh. No one dared to venture near the haunted spot after sun-

set, and all those who could avoided it in the daytime, and travelers were warned of the dreaded place.

One day as the sun was setting, a priest came to the plain. He was a belated traveler, and his robe showed that he was a Buddhist pilgrim walking from shrine to shrine to pray for some blessing or to crave for forgiveness of sins. He had apparently lost his way, and as it was late he met no one who could show him the road or warn him of the haunted spot.

He had walked the whole day and was now tired and hungry, and the evenings were chilly, for it was late autumn, and he began to be very anxious to find some house where he could obtain a night's lodging. He found himself lost in the midst of the large plain, and looked about in vain for some sign of human habitation.

At last, after wandering about for some hours, he saw a clump of trees in the distance, and through the trees he caught sight of the glimmer of a single ray of light. He exclaimed with joy:

"Oh, surely that is some cottage where I can get a night's lodging!"

Keeping the light before his eyes, he dragged his weary, aching feet as quickly as he could towards the spot, and soon came to a miserable-looking little cottage. As he drew near he saw that it was in a tumble-down condition, the bamboo fence was broken and weeds and grass pushed their way through the gaps. The paper screens which serve as windows and doors in Japan were full of holes, and the posts of the house were bent with age and seemed scarcely able to support the old thatched roof. The hut was open, and by the light of an old lantern an old woman sat industriously spinning.

The pilgrim called to her across the bamboo fence and said:

"O Baa San (old woman), good evening! I am a traveler! Please excuse me, but I have lost my way and do not know what to do, for I have nowhere to rest tonight. I beg you to be good enough to let me spend the night under your roof."

The old woman as soon as she heard herself spoken to stopped spinning, rose from her seat and approached the intruder.

"I am very sorry for you. You must indeed be distressed to have lost your way in such a lonely spot so late at night. Unfortunately I cannot put you up, for I have no bed to offer you, and no accommodation whatsoever for a guest in this poor place!"

"Oh, that does not matter," said the priest, "all I want is a shelter under some roof for the night, and if you will be good enough just to let me lie on the kitchen floor I shall be grateful. I am too tired to walk further to-night, so I hope you will not refuse me, otherwise I shall have to sleep out on the cold plain." And in this way he pressed the old woman to let him stay.

She seemed very reluctant, but at last she said:

"Very well, I will let you stay here. I can offer you a very poor welcome only, but come in now and I will make a fire, for the night is cold."

The pilgrim was only too glad to do as he was told. He took off his sandals and entered the hut. The old woman then brought some sticks of wood and lit the fire, and bade her guest draw near and warm himself.

"You must be hungry after your long tramp," said the old woman. "I will go and cook some supper for you." She then went to the kitchen to cook some rice.

After the priest had finished his supper the old woman sat down by the fire-place, and they talked together for a long time. The pilgrim thought to himself that he had been very lucky to come across such a kind, hospitable old woman. At last the wood gave out, and as the fire died slowly down he began to shiver with cold just as he had done when he arrived.

"I see you are cold," said the old woman. "I will go out and gather some wood, for we have used it all. You must stay and take care of the house while I am gone."

"No, no," said the pilgrim, "let me go instead, for you are old, and I cannot think of letting you go out to get wood for me this cold night!"

The old woman shook her head and said:

"You must stay quietly here, for you are my guest." Then she left him and went out.

In a minute she came back and said:

"You must sit where you are and not move, and whatever happens don't go near or look into the inner room. Now mind what I tell you!"

"If you tell me not to go near the back room, of course I won't," said the priest, rather bewildered.

The old woman then went out again, and the priest was left alone. The fire had died out, and the only light in the hut was that of a dim lantern. For the first time that night he began to feel that he was in a weird place, and the old woman's words, "Whatever you do don't peep into the back room," aroused his curiosity and his fear.

What hidden thing could be in that room that she did not wish him to see? For some time the remembrance of his promise to the old woman kept him still, but at last he could no longer resist his curiosity to peep into the forbidden place.

He got up and began to move slowly towards the back room. Then the thought that the old woman would be very angry with him if he disobeyed her made him come back to his place by the fireside.

As the minutes went slowly by and the old woman did not return, he began to feel more and more frightened, and to wonder what dreadful secret was in the room behind him. He must find out.

"She will not know that I have looked unless I tell her. I will just have a peep before she comes back," said the man to himself.

With these words he got up on his feet (for he had been sitting all this time in Japanese fashion with his feet under him) and stealthily crept towards the forbidden spot. With trembling hands he pushed back the sliding door and looked in. What he saw froze the blood in his veins. The room was full of dead men's bones and the walls were splashed and the floor was covered with human blood. In one corner skull upon skull rose to the ceiling, in another was a heap of arm bones, in another a heap of leg bones. The sickening smell made him faint. He fell backwards with horror, and for some time lay in a heap with fright on the floor, a pitiful sight.

He trembled all over and his teeth chattered, and he could hardly crawl away from the dreadful spot.

He trembled all over and his teeth chattered, and he could hardly crawl away from the dreadful spot.

"How horrible!" he cried out. "What awful den have I come to in my travels? May Buddha help me or I am lost. Is it possible that that kind old woman is really the cannibal goblin? When she comes back she will show herself in her true character and eat me up at one mouthful!"

With these words his strength came back to him and, snatching up his hat and staff, he rushed out of the house as fast as his legs could carry him. Out into the night he ran, his one thought to get as far as he could from the goblin's haunt. He had not gone far when he heard steps behind him and a voice crying: "Stop! Stop!"

He ran on, redoubling his speed, pretending not to hear. As he ran he heard the steps behind him come nearer and nearer, and at last he recognized the old woman's voice which grew louder and louder as she came nearer.

"Stop! Stop, you wicked man, why did you look into the forbidden room?"

The priest quite forgot how tired he was and his feet flew over the ground faster than ever. Fear gave him strength, for he knew that if the goblin caught him he would soon be one of her victims. With all his heart he repeated the prayer to Buddha:

"Namu Amida Butsu, Namu Amida Butsu."

And after him rushed the dreadful old hag, her hair flying in the wind, and her face changing with rage into the demon that she was. In her hand she carried a large blood-stained knife, and she still shrieked after him, "Stop! Stop!"

At last, when the priest felt he could run no more, the dawn broke, and with the darkness of night the goblin vanished and he was safe. The priest now knew that he had met the Goblin of Adachigahara, the story of whom he had often heard but never believed to be true. He felt that he owed his wonderful escape to the protection of Buddha to whom he had prayed for help, so he took out his rosary and, bowing his head as the sun rose, he said his prayers and made his thanksgiving earnestly. He then set forward for another part of the country, only too glad to leave the haunted plain behind him.

The Hopskinville Goblins

In 1955, eleven members of two families living in a rural farmhouse between Kelly and Hopskinville, Kentucky, reported numerous encounters with unidentifiable creatures. In addition to lights and odd noises heard by witnesses nearby, the families claimed that they were terrorized by little creatures similar to goblins or fearsome gremlins. They were described as being three feet tall, thin, with long arms and claw-like hands, and with pointed ears. They were silvery in color and were said to float, trudge as though underwater, and then make sudden appearances outside windows and doorways. Although at first two members of the party had attempted to shoot and then find them, eventually they retreated to the house. The creatures did not enter the house (the family dog was hiding underneath in terror) but they continued to appear throughout the evening. Ultimately the families, including screaming children, made a midnight dash to the police station. Here's where it gets weird: the families returned to the farmhouse with the sheriff and twenty of his men. Evidence of struggle and damage to the house was obvious, but the officers reported seeing a strange green glow at the edge of the woods beyond the property. They interviewed neighbors who affirmed odd noises and lights, and even the police saw strange lights and heard odd noises while at the property. After the police left, the creatures returned and continued to harass the family until the break of day, when they disappeared, never to return again.

Fiddle Me This

"The Magic Fiddle" comes to us by way of a collection called *Indian Fairy Tales*, gathered by Joseph Jacobs and published in 1912. Jacobs (1854–1916) was an

Australian scholar who cited the Brothers Grimm as his influence in collecting the forgotten fairy tales. In addition to *Indian Fairy Tales*, Jacobs also collected and published many other volumes, including *English Fairy Tales*, *Celtic Folk and Fairy Tales*, and *European Folk and Fairy Tales*.

The fairy-like spirit in this story, the bonga, is often identified as a malevolent spirit that does the bidding of witches. This story implies that almost anyone can have a bonga that they can call upon (or are the wives witches?). Most scholars agree that a bonga is meant to be mischievous at minimum and is not unlike a trickster sprite. The following story features a *jogi*, which refers to a Hindu *Fakir* (devotee) or sometimes a caste of Hindu who are commonly weavers. Interestingly, a *jogini* is often defined as a female fiend or sprite, attending to or created by a *Durga* (deity).

Although some may view this as a story of triumph, it demonstrates the matter-of-fact nature of spirits to destroy and to reinvent. The victim in this case is reinvented more than once, from human to bonga, bonga to bamboo, and bamboo to fiddle. It also strikes a chord (ha ha!) of resemblance to the

Celtic tale of the two sisters, in which revenge is delivered by the confession of a musical instrument.

The Magic Fiddle

by Joseph Jacobs, Ed.

Once upon a time there lived seven brothers and a sister. The brothers were married, but their wives did not do the cooking for the family. It was done by their sister, who stopped at home to cook. The wives for this reason bore their sister-in-law much ill-will, and at length they combined together to oust her from the office of cook and general provider, so that one of themselves might obtain it. They said, "She does not go out to the fields to work, but remains quietly at home, and yet she has not the meals ready at the proper time."

They then called upon their bonga, and vowing vows unto him they secured his good-will and assistance; then they said to the bonga, "At midday when our sister-in-law goes to bring water, cause it thus to happen, that on seeing her pitcher the water shall vanish, and again slowly reappear. In this way she will be delayed. Let the water not flow into her pitcher, and you may keep the maiden as your own."

At noon when she went to bring water, it suddenly dried up before her, and she began to weep. Then after a while the water began slowly to rise. When it reached her ankles she tried to fill her pitcher, but it would not go under the water. Being frightened she began to wail and cry to her brother:

"Oh! my brother, the water reaches to my ankles, still. Oh! my brother, the pitcher will not dip."

The water continued to rise until it reached her knee, when she began to wail again:

"Oh! my brother, the water reaches to my knee, still. Oh! my brother, the pitcher will not dip."

The water continued to rise, and when it reached her waist, she cried again:

"Oh! my brother, the water reaches to my waist, still. Oh! my brother, the pitcher will not dip."

The water still rose, and when it reached her neck she kept on crying:

"Oh! my brother, the water reaches to my neck, still. Oh! my brother, the pitcher will not dip."

At length the water became so deep that she felt herself drowning, then she cried aloud:

"Oh! my brother, the water measures a man's height. Oh! my brother, the pitcher begins to fill."

The pitcher filled with water, and along with it she sank and was drowned. The bonga then transformed her into a bonga like himself, and carried her off.

After a time she re-appeared as a bamboo growing on the embankment of the tank in which she had been drowned. When the bamboo had grown to an immense size, a jogi, who was in the habit of passing that way, seeing it, said to himself, "This will make a splendid fiddle."

So one day he brought an axe to cut it down; but when he was about to begin, the bamboo called out, "Do not cut at the root, cut higher up."

When he lifted his axe to cut high up the stem, the bamboo cried out, "Do not cut near the top, cut at the root."

When the jogi again prepared himself to cut at the root as requested, the bamboo said, "Do not cut at the root, cut higher up," and when he was about to cut higher up, it again called out to him, "Do not cut high up, cut at the root."

The jogi by this time felt sure that a bonga was trying to frighten him, so becoming angry he cut down the bamboo at the root, and taking it away made a fiddle out of it. The instrument had a superior tone and delighted all who heard it. The jogi carried it with him when he went a-begging, and through the influence of its sweet music he returned home every evening with a full wallet.

He now and then visited, when on his rounds, the house of the bonga girl's brothers, and the strains of the fiddle affected them greatly. Some of them were moved even to tears, for the fiddle seemed to wail as one in bitter anguish. The elder brother wished to purchase it, and offered to support the jogi for a whole year if he would consent to part with his wonderful instrument. The jogi, however, knew its value, and refused to sell it.

It so happened that the jogi some time after went to the house of a village chief, and after playing a tune or two on his fiddle asked for something to eat. They offered to buy his fiddle and promised a high price for it, but he refused to sell it, as his fiddle brought to him his means of livelihood. When they saw that he was not to be prevailed upon, they gave him food and a plentiful supply of liquor. Of the latter he drank so freely that he presently became intoxicated. While he was in this condition, they took away his fiddle, and substituted their own old one for it. When the jogi recovered, he missed his instrument, and suspecting that it had been stolen asked them to return it to him. They denied having taken it, so he had to depart, leaving his fiddle behind him.

The chief's son, being a musician, used to play on the jogi's fiddle, and in his hands the music it gave forth delighted the ears of all who heard it.

When all the household were absent at their labours in the fields, the bonga girl used to come out of the bamboo fiddle, and prepared the family meal. Having eaten her own share, she placed that of the chief's son under his bed, and covering it up to keep off the dust, re-entered the fiddle. This happening every day, the other members of the household thought that some girl friend of theirs was in this manner showing her interest in the young man, so they did not trouble themselves to find out how it came about. The young chief, however, was determined to watch, and see which of his girl friends was so attentive to his comfort. He said in his own mind, "I will catch her today, and give her a sound beating; she is causing me to be ashamed before the others." So saying, he hid himself in a corner in a pile of firewood. In a short time the girl came out of the bamboo fiddle, and began to dress her hair. Having completed her toilet, she cooked the meal of rice as usual, and having eaten some herself, she placed the young man's portion under his bed, as before, and was about to enter the fiddle again, when he, running out from his hiding-place, caught her in his arms. The bonga girl exclaimed, "Fie! Fie! you may be a Dom, or you may be a Hadi of some other caste with whom I cannot marry." He said, "No. But from today, you and I are one." So they began lovingly to hold converse with each other. When the others returned home in the evening, they saw that she was both a human being and a bonga, and they rejoiced exceedingly.

Now in course of time the bonga girl's family became very poor, and her brothers on one occasion came to the chief's house on a visit.

The bonga girl recognised them at once, but they did not know who she was. She brought them water on their arrival, and afterwards set cooked rice before them. Then sitting down near them, she began in wailing tones to upbraid them on account of the treatment she had been subjected to by their wives. She related all that had befallen her, and wound up by saying, "You must have known it all, and yet you did not interfere to save me." And that was all the revenge she took.

Trolls

Trolls, you may think, live strictly under bridges. While this is a very popular place for them, they can be found in caves, mountain dwellings, and other areas where they cannot be easily spotted, as they are often larger than their fairy counterparts. Not all trolls are male.

Sometimes the terms troll and dwarf or even elf are used interchangeably in old stories, but the evolved troll of today is larger, uglier, and somewhat shyer than the troll of yesteryear.

The *Huldra,* or in Sweden the *Tallemaja,* is a fair and beautiful troll woman who has a long cow-tail. She, like many trolls, is neither bad nor good.

Sometimes the terms troll and dwarf or even elf are used interchangeably in old stories, but the evolved troll of today is larger, uglier, and somewhat shyer than the troll of yesteryear.

For Whom the Bridge Trolls

It lives under the north end of the George Washington Memorial Bridge, aka the Aurora Bridge. Four local Seattle artists, Donna Walter, Ross Whitehead, Steve Badanes, and Will Martin, created the eighteen-foot-high sculpture out of concrete, rebar, and wire in 1990. The troll was installed in response to the area under the bridge becoming a haven for drug use and drug dealers. Now the troll resides, holding up a VW Bug, for all to see and to feel. You can climb on it and if you find yourself in Seattle, you must snap your photo with it.

After the 1989 Loma Prieta earthquake struck the San Francisco Bay Area, the eastern span of the Bay Bridge suffered major damage. When being repaired, Bill Roan, a blacksmith and artist, made a troll that ironworkers snuck onto the bridge and welded into place. In 2013, the segment of the Bay Bridge that was home to the infamous Bay Bridge troll was dismantled and the troll was taken down, much to the dismay of citizens of the area. He was put on display at the Oakland Museum of California and has since made the rounds in numerous local art exhibits. He is surprisingly small in stature.

In Norway, trolls are believed to disappear as balls of yarn. In the following story, the trolls use their powers of enchantment to try to take a bride and use their powers of the skein to make a hasty departure. Luckily for the trolls in this story, from Clara Stroebe's *The Norwegian Fairy Book*, no kittens were about.

The Troll Wedding

edited by Clara Stroebe

One summer, a long, long time ago, the folk of Melbustad went up to the hill pastures with their herd. But they had been there only a short time when the cattle began to grow so restless that it was impossible to keep them in order. A number of different maidens tried to manage them, but without avail; until one came who was betrothed, and whose betrothal had but recently been celebrated. Then the cattle suddenly quieted down, and were easy to handle. So the maiden remained alone in the hills with no other company than a dog. And one afternoon as she sat in the hut, it seemed to her that her sweetheart came, sat down beside her, and began to talk about their getting married at once. But she sat still and made no reply, for she noticed a strangeness about him. By and by, more and more people came in, and they began to cover the table with silverware, and bring on dishes, and the bridesmaids brought the bridal crown, and the ornaments, and a handsome bridal gown, and they dressed her, and put the crown on her head, as was the custom in those days, and they put rings on her hands.

And it seemed to her as though she knew all the people who were there; they were the women of the

village, and the girls of her own age. But the dog was well aware that there was something uncanny about it all. He made his way down to Melbustad in flying leaps, and howled and barked in the most lamentable manner, and gave the people no rest until they followed him. The young fellow who was to marry the girl took his gun, and climbed the hills; and when he drew near, there stood a number of horses around the hut, saddled and bridled. He crept up to the hut, looked through a loop-hole in the wall, and saw a whole company sitting together inside. It was quite evident that they were trolls, the people from underground, and therefore he discharged his gun over the roof. At that moment the doors flew open, and a number of balls of gray yarn, one larger than the other, came shooting out about his legs. When he went in, there sat the maiden in her bridal finery, and nothing was missing but the ring on her little finger, then all would have been complete.

"In heaven's name, what has happened here?" he

asked, as he looked around. All the silverware was still on the table, but all the tasty dishes had turned to moss and toadstools, and frogs and toads and the like.

"What does it all mean?" said he. "You are sitting here in all your glory, just like a bride?"

"How can you ask me?" answered the maiden. "You have been sitting here yourself, and talking about our wedding the whole afternoon!"

"No, I have just come," said he. "It must have been someone else who had taken my shape!"

Then she gradually came to her senses; but not until long afterward was she altogether herself, and she told how she had firmly believed that her sweetheart himself, and all their friends and relatives had been there. He took her straight back to the village with him, and so that they need fear no such deviltry in the future, they celebrated their wedding while she was still clad in the bridal outfit of the underground folk. The crown and all the ornaments were hung up in Melbustad and it is said that they hang there to this very day.

The Fairies

by William Allingham

Up the airy mountain,
Down the rushy glen,
We daren't go a-hunting
For fear of little men;
Wee folk, good folk,
Trooping all together;
Green jacket, red cap,
And white owl's feather!

Down along the rocky shore
Some make their home,
They live on crispy pancakes
Of yellow tide-foam;
Some in the reeds
Of the black mountain lake,
With frogs for their watch-dogs
All night awake.

High on the hill-top
The old King sits;
He is now so old and gray
He's nigh lost his wits.
With a bridge of white mist
Columbkill he crosses,

On his stately journeys
From Slieveleague to Rosses;
Or going up with music
On cold starry nights,
To sup with the Queen
Of the gay Northern Lights.

They stole little Bridget
For seven years long;
When she came down again
Her friends were all gone.
They took her lightly back,
Between the night and morrow,
They thought that she was fast asleep,
But she was dead with sorrow.
They have kept her ever since
Deep within the lake,
On a bed of flag-leaves,
till she wake.

By the craggy hill-side,
Through the mosses bare,
They have planted thorn-trees
For pleasure here and there.
Is any man so daring
As dig them up in spite,

He shall find their sharpest thorns
In his bed at night.

Up the airy mountain,
Down the rushy glen,
We daren't go a-hunting
For fear of little men;
Wee folk, good folk,
Trooping all together;
Green jacket, red cap,
And white owl's feather!

Chapter 2
The Hand That Rocks the Cradle

Changelings and Other Greedy Kidnappers of the Fairy Kingdom

Sleep, my child! for the rustling trees,
Stirr'd by the breath of summer breeze,
And fairy songs of sweetest note,
Around us gently float.

J. J. CALLANAN, TRANSLATED FROM THE IRISH

Of all the things that creep about beneath the leaves and shuffle between the shadows, there are few things that bring a shiver to the spine like the idea of a changeling. A parent's worst fear is harm coming to your child. Imagine, then, a young mother, exhausted from a long, hard labor and slipping into a moment of sleep, her newborn child bundled carefully in a cradle by the bedside. There's a fire in the hearth and a candle flickering on the table. Now imagine she wakes suddenly: the candle is snuffed out and the fire but ash and a few embers. She reaches for her sweet babe, who has begun to cry—a most wretched sound unlike a noise she's ever heard.

As she lifts her child to her breast she sees not the apple cheeks and soft lines of a precious new baby, but rather something wriggling, writhing with beady eyes and a peculiar scent.

As she lifts her child to her breast she sees not the apple cheeks and soft lines of a precious new baby, but rather something wriggling, writhing with beady eyes and a peculiar scent. She holds in her arms a changeling: a child switched for her own by malicious fairies who love nothing more than the beautiful children of mortals.

Sometimes the fairies fancy mortals, and carry them away into their own country, leaving instead some sickly fairy child, or a log of wood so bewitched that it seems to be a mortal pining away, and dying, and being buried. Most commonly they steal children. If you "over look a child," that is look on it with envy, the fairies have it in their power.

W. B. YEATS, *FAIRY AND FOLK TALES OF THE IRISH PEASANTRY*

Today's parent is an informed parent. From checkups to child locks, the modern mom and dad do everything they can to ensure their little one will be safe and happy. So it is a shame that so many parents are completely unaware of one of the biggest threats to babies out there: fairies. Yes, babies are of particular interest to fairies, and the wicked fae will often stop at nothing to get their hands on a precious little bundle.

Many a parent has been tricked by the Queen of the Fairies, whose orders result in switching a creature from another realm for their human counterpart. When a sweet and robust baby goes ill, losing cheerful demeanor and coloring, perhaps developing a nasty cough that rattles the cradle, that is the sign of a changeling. When a calm and cuddly newborn becomes

fussy and cries all hours of the night, it isn't colic, as so many foolish parents suspect. It is much more likely to be the offspring of a foul troll or lovely pixie, switched with the sleeping babe while the exhausted parents slumbered.

William Butler Yeats collected such stories from all over Ireland in the late 1800s, primarily from the peasant class, where folklore and the old ways taught people how to live in harmonious fear of the dangerous fairy folk. In this collection, we'll find excerpts from Yeats and T. Crofton Croker, among others, all regarding ways in which the little people and fairy folk have craftily, cunningly tricked mortals into giving up or sacrificing their own kin.

It is a dreadful thought, but one that is difficult to deny. Who is that sleeping innocently in your arms? You may never know—at least, not until it's too late!

And lest you childless ones think you are safe, or those whose children have grown to adulthood, it should be noted that fairies *prefer* babies and children. However, they have been known to trick and entice grown adults if no children are available. So don't think you are going to sleep easy every night just because you don't have to worry about kidnapping. And the fairy folk don't offer ransom. You'll be trapped in their world, which maybe doesn't seem so bad in theory. But night after night of dancing and revelry can wear out even the toughest rock star. So be warned!

Jane Wilde, the mother of Oscar Wilde, was a writer and poet who published intel on the Irish fairies and associated folk magic. She offers sound advice on the prevention of changelings:

> When a woman first takes ill in her confine-
> ment, unlock instantly every press and drawer
> in the house, but when the child is born, lock
> them all up again at once, for if care is not
> taken the fairies will get in and hide in the
> drawers and presses, to be ready to steal away
> the little mortal baby when they get the oppor-
> tunity, and place some ugly, wizened change-
> ling in the cradle beside the poor mother.
> Therefore every key should be turned, every
> lock made fast; and if the fairies are hidden
> inside, let them stay there until the danger is
> over for the baby by the proper precautions
> being taken, such as a red coal set under
> the cradle, and a branch of the moun-
> tain ash tied over it, or of the alder-
> tree, according to the sex of the child, for
> both trees have mystic virtues, probably

because of the ancient superstition that the first man was created from an alder-tree, and the first woman from the mountain ash.

Should the fairies manage to carry off someone you love, take heart. Vigilant mothers have been known to find the baby before it has been carried far and simply take it back. Occasionally a kind-hearted fairy will return the human child. You can try setting the crying child outside, in the hopes that the fairy mother will come and wish to comfort their own child. There are also some more desperate measures you can take. Get your oven nice and hot, and then have a friend or nurse-maid ask you loudly three times, "Why are you making the oven so hot?" And each time answer, "Why, to burn my child in it to death." Upon saying it the third time the fairy folk will appear, switch back your real baby and never return. Brutal, but again, desperate times.

There are stories of families who go on to raise the changeling as one of their own. The child has, not surprisingly, a terrible temperament, but is also gifted in the arts, especially music. Changeling children have been known to try and kill or at least bring harm to their parents. And since we've already gone down this dark and loathsome path, I will make no attempt to reassure you who have grown children or who are grown adults yourself. Sometimes fairies snatch older children, beautiful people, or full-grown mortals who seem appealing to them.

As Yeats writes:

Many things can be done to find out in a child a changeling, but there is one infallible thing—lay it on the fire with this formula, "Burn, burn, burn—if of the devil, burn; but if of God and the saints, be safe from harm" (given by Lady Wilde). Then if it be a changeling it will rush up the chimney with a cry, for, according to Giraldus Cambrensis, "fire is the greatest of enemies to every sort of phantom, in so much that those who have seen apparitions fall into a swoon as soon as they are sensible of the brightness of fire."

Sometimes the creature is got rid of in a more gentle way. It is on record that once when a mother was leaning over a wizened changeling the latch lifted and a fairy came in, carrying home again the wholesome stolen baby. "It was the others," she said, "who stole it." As for her, she wanted her own child.

Those who are carried away are happy, according to some accounts, having plenty of good living and music and mirth. Others say, however, that they are continually longing for their earthly friends.

Lady Wilde gives a gloomy tradition that there are two kinds of fairies—one kind, merry, and gentle, the other evil and sacrificing every year a life to Satan, for which purpose they steal mortals.

> *Lady Wilde gives a gloomy tradition that there are two kinds of fairies—one kind, merry, and gentle, the other evil, and sacrificing every year a life to Satan, for which purpose they steal mortals.*

No other Irish writer gives this tradition—if such fairies there be, they must be among the solitary spirits—pookas, fir darrigs, and the like.

Here's a sad and odd little tale of a how a couple got rid of a changeling from W. Y. Evans-Wentz's *The Fairy-Faith in Celtic Countries*. Their method was unusual but, alas, their own child was not returned to them.

The Changeling

by W. Y. Evans-Wentz

There lived once, near Tiis lake, two lonely people, who were sadly plagued with a changeling, given them by the underground-people instead of their own child. This changeling behaved in a very strange and uncommon manner, for when there was no one in the place, he was in great spirits, ran up the walls like a cat, sat under the roof, and shouted and bawled away lustily; but sat dozing at the end of the table when any one was in the room with him. He was able to eat as much as any four, and never cared what it was that was set before him; but though he regarded not the quality of his food, in quantity he was never satisfied, and gave excessive annoyance to everyone in the house.

When they had tried for a long time in vain how they could best get rid of him, since there was no living in the house with him, a smart girl pledged herself that she would banish him from the house. She accordingly, while he was out in the fields, took a pig and killed it, and put it, hide, hair, and all, into a black pudding, and set it before him when he came home. He began, as was his custom, to gobble it up, but when he had eaten for some time, he began to relax a little in his efforts, and at last he sat quite still, with his knife in his hand, looking at the pudding.

At length, after sitting for some time in this manner, he began, "A pudding with hide!—and a pudding with hair! a pudding with eyes!—and a pudding with legs in it! Well, three times have I seen a young wood by Tiis lake, but never yet did I see such a pudding! The devil himself may stay here now for me!" So saying, he ran off with himself, and never more came back again.

To Cure a Fairy-Stricken Child

Make a good fire, throw into it a handful or more of certain herbs ordered by the fairy-women; wait till a great smoke rises, then carry the child three times round the fire, reciting an incantation against evil, and sprinkling holy water all around. But during the process no door must be opened, or the fairies would come in to see what you are doing. Continue reciting the incantation till the child sneezes three times; then you may know that the fairy spell is broken, and the child redeemed from fairy thraldom for evermore . . .

Lady Wilde

Shell Shock

It appears also that eggs play a role in the crusade against changelings. When I first read this story by T. Crofton Croker (there is more on this Irish native in chapter three), I was not clear on the significance of the eggshells in the brew that the mother makes, as I had not read before of such a remedy to banish a change-ling. And then I came upon this part of a poem by Dora Sigerson (Shorter):

"From the speckled hen nine eggs I stole,
And lighting a fire of a glowing coal,
I fried the shells, and I spilt the yolk;
But never a word the stranger spoke."

The poem goes on to describe the previously men-tioned red-hot poker method. The cooking of the egg-shells seems to be an important step.

The Brewery of Eggshells

by T. Crofton Croker

It may be considered impertinent, were I to explain what is meant by a changeling; both Shakespeare and Spenser have already done so, and who is there unac-quainted *A Mid-summer Night's Dream* and *The Fairy Queen*.

Now Mrs. Sullivan fancied that her youngest child had been changed by "fairies' theft," to use Spenser's words, and certainly appearances warranted such a conclusion; for in one night her healthy, blue-eyed boy had become shrivelled up into almost nothing, and never ceased squalling and crying. This naturally made poor Mrs. Sullivan very unhappy; and all the neighbours, by way of comforting her, said that her own child was, beyond any kind of doubt, with the good people, and that one of themselves had been put in his place.

Mrs. Sullivan, of course, could not disbelieve what everyone told her, but she did not wish to hurt the thing; for although its face was so withered, and its body wasted away to a mere skeleton, it had still a strong resemblance to her own boy; she, therefore, could not find it in her heart to roast it alive on the griddle, or to burn its nose off with the red-hot tongs, or to throw it out in the snow on the road-side, notwithstanding these, and several like proceedings, were strongly recommended to her for the recovery of her child.

One day who should Mrs. Sullivan meet but a cunning woman, well known about the country by the name of Ellen Leah (or Gray Ellen). She had the gift, however she got it, of telling where the dead were, and what was good for the rest of their souls; and could charm away warts and wens, and do a great many wonderful things of the same nature.

"You're in grief this morning, Mrs. Sullivan," were the first words of Ellen Leah to her.

"You may say that, Ellen," said Mrs. Sullivan, "and good cause I have to be in grief, for there was my own fine child whipped off from me out of his cradle, without as much as by your leave, or ask your pardon, and an ugly dony bit of a shrivelled-up fairy put in his place: no wonder then that you see me in grief, Ellen."

"Small blame to you, Mrs. Sullivan," said Ellen Leah, "but are you sure 'tis a fairy?"

"Sure!" echoed Mrs. Sullivan, "sure enough am I to my sorrow, and can I doubt my own two eyes? Every mother's soul must feel for me!"

"Will you take an old woman's advice?" said Ellen Leah, fixing her wild and mysterious gaze upon the unhappy mother; and, after a pause, she added, "but maybe you'll call it foolish?"

"Can you get me back my child,—my own child, Ellen?" said Mrs. Sullivan with great energy.

"If you do as I bid you," returned Ellen Leah, "you'll know." Mrs. Sullivan was silent in expectation, and Ellen continued. "Put down the big pot, full of water, on the fire, and make it boil like mad; then get a dozen new-laid eggs, break them, and keep the shells, but throw away the rest; when that is done, put the shells in the pot of boiling water, and you will soon know whether it is your own boy or a fairy."

"If you find that it is a fairy in the cradle, take the red-hot poker and cram it down his ugly throat, and you will not have much trouble with him after that, I promise you."

Home went Mrs. Sullivan, and did as Ellen Leah desired. She put the pot in the fire, and plenty of turf under it, and set the water boiling at such a rate that if ever water was red hot—it surely was.

The child was lying for a wonder quite easy and quiet in the cradle, every now and then cocking his eye, that would twinkle as keen as a star in a frosty night, over at the great fire, and the big pot upon it; and he looked on with great attention at Mrs. Sullivan breaking the eggs, and putting down the egg-shells to boil. At last he asked, with the voice of a very old man, "What are you doing, mammy?"

> "If you find that it is a fairy in the cradle, take the red-hot poker and cram it down his ugly throat, and you will not have much trouble with him after that, I promise you."

Mrs. Sullivan's heart, as she said herself, was up in her mouth ready to choke her, at hearing the child speak. But she contrived to put the poker in the fire, and to answer, without making any wonder at the words, "I'm brewing, *a vick*" (my son).

"And what are you brewing, mammy?" said the little imp, whose supernatural gift of speech now proved beyond question that he was a fairy substitute.

"I wish the poker was red," thought Mrs. Sullivan; but it was a large one, and took a long time heating: so she determined to keep him in talk until the poker was in a proper state to thrust down his throat, and therefore repeated the question.

"Is it what I'm brewing, *a vick*," said she, "you want to know?"

"Yes, mammy: what are you brewing?" returned the fairy.

"Egg-shells, *a vick*," said Mrs. Sullivan.

"Oh!" shrieked the imp, starting up in the cradle, and clapping his hands together, "I'm fifteen hundred years in the world, and I never saw a brewery of egg-shells before!" The poker was by this time quite red, and Mrs. Sullivan seizing it, ran furiously towards the cradle; but somehow or other her foot slipped, and she fell flat on the floor, and the poker flew out of her hand to the other end of the house. However, she got up, without much loss of time, and went to the cradle intending to pitch the wicked thing that was in it into the pot of boiling water, when there she saw her own child in a sweet sleep, one of his soft round arms rested upon the pillow—his features were as placid as if their repose had never been disturbed, save the rosy mouth which moved with a gentle and regular breathing.

Who can tell the feelings of a mother when she looks upon her sleeping child? Why should I, therefore, endeavour to describe those of Mrs. Sullivan at again beholding her long-lost boy? The fountain of her heart overflowed with the excess of joy—and she wept!—tears trickled silently down her cheeks, nor did she strive to check them—they were tears not of sorrow, but of happiness.

The Fairy Nurse by Edward Walsh

Sweet babe! a golden cradle holds thee, And soft the snow-white fleece enfolds thee; In airy bower I'll watch thy sleeping, Where branchy trees to the breeze are sweeping.

Shuheen, sho, lulo lo!

When mothers languish broken-hearted, When young wives are from husbands parted, Ah! little think the keeners lonely, They weep some time-worn fairy only.

Shuheen sho, lulo lo!

Within our magic halls of brightness, Trips many a foot of snowy whiteness; Stolen maidens, queens of fairy—And kings and chiefs a sluagh-shee airy,

Shuheen sho, lulo lo!

Rest thee, babe! I love thee dearly, And as thy mortal mother nearly; Ours is the swiftest steed and proudest, That moves where the tramp of the host is loudest.

Shuheen sho, lulo lo!

Rest thee, babe! for soon thy slumbers Shall flee at the magic koelshie's numbers; In airy

bower I'll watch thy sleeping, Where branchy trees to the breeze are sweeping.
Shuheen sho, lulo, lo!

Every Day Is Halloween

If you don't remember the Ministry song that bears the above title, I can only say more's the pity, but since no one is perfect I won't hold that against you. The next story illustrates a delightful (and frightful) connection between Halloween and the magic of the little people. It is no surprise that today's practice of dressing up like all manner of creatures has its roots in the belief that All Hallow's Eve was a time when such wild beasties ran amok. In order to pass among them, people would dress in masks and strange attire.

Trick or treating, in which human "little people" perform impish antics if they don't receive their treats, echoes the vengeful brownie or house imp who didn't get the freshest cakes.

In Jamie Freel's case, the kidnapping—which is not of a child—is first done by the wee folk, but then again by our hero, who manages to outwit the little men and women more than once. The author, Miss Letitia McClintock (sometimes referred to as Mrs. Maclintock, the spelling of which appears to be incorrect), was a Donegal writer who wrote throughout the 1870s and 1880s. Her work was favored by Yeats.

Jamie Freel and the Young Lady

A Donegal Tale by Letitia McClintock

Down in Fannet, in times gone by, lived Jamie Freel and his mother. Jamie was the widow's sole support; his strong arm worked for her untiringly, and as each Saturday night came round, he poured his wages into her lap, thanking her dutifully for the halfpence which she returned him for tobacco.

He was extolled by his neighbors as the best son ever known or heard of. But he had neighbors of whose opinion he was ignorant—neighbors who lived pretty close to him, whom he had never seen, who are, indeed, rarely seen by mortals, except on May eves and Halloweens.

An old ruined castle, about a quarter of a mile from his cabin, was said to be the abode of the "wee folk." Every Halloween were the ancient windows lighted up, and passers-by saw little figures flitting to and fro inside the building, while they heard the music of pipes and flutes.

It was well known that fairy revels took place; but nobody had the courage to intrude on them.

Jamie had often watched the little figures from a distance, and listened to the charming music, wondering what the inside of the castle was like; but one Halloween he got up and took his cap, saying to his mother, "I'm awa' to the castle to seek my fortune."

"What!" cried she, "would you venture there? You that's the poor widow's one son! Dinna be so venturesome and foolish, Jamie! They'll kill you, and then what'll come o' me?"

"Never fear, mother; no harm 'ill happen me, but I must go."

He set out, and as he crossed the potato-field, came in sight of the castle, whose windows were ablaze with light, that seemed to turn the russet leaves, still clinging to the crabtree branches, into gold.

Halting in the grove at one side of the ruin, he listened to the elfin revelry, and the laughter and singing made him all the more determined to proceed.

Numbers of little people, the largest about the size of a child of five years old, were dancing to the music of flutes and fiddles, while others drank and feasted.

"Welcome, Jamie Freel! Welcome, welcome, Jamie!" cried the company, perceiving their visitor. The word "Welcome" was caught up and repeated by every voice in the castle.

Time flew, and Jamie was enjoying himself very much, when his hosts said, "We're going to ride to Dublin to-night to steal a young lady. Will you come too, Jamie Freel?"

"Ay, that will I!" cried the rash youth, thirsting for adventure.

A troop of horses stood at the door. Jamie mounted, and his steed rose with him into the air. He was presently flying over his mother's cottage, surrounded by the elfin troop, and on and on they went, over bold mountains, over little hills, over the deep Lough Swilley, over towns and cottages, when people were burning nuts, and eating apples, and keeping merry Halloween. It seemed to Jamie that they flew all round Ireland before they got to Dublin.

"This is Derry," said the fairies, flying over the cathedral spire; and what was said by one voice was repeated by all the rest, till fifty little voices were crying out, "Derry! Derry! Derry!"

In like manner was Jamie informed as they passed over each town on the route, and at length he heard the silvery voices cry, "Dublin! Dublin!"

It was no mean dwelling that was to be honored by the fairy visit, but one of the finest houses in Stephen's Green.

The troop dismounted near a window, and Jamie saw a beautiful face, on a pillow in a splendid bed. He saw the young lady lifted and carried away, while the stick which was dropped in her place on the bed took her exact form.

The lady was placed before one rider and carried a short way, then given another, and the names of the towns were cried out as before.

They were approaching home. Jamie heard "Rathmullan," "Milford," "Tamney," and then he knew they were near his own house.

"You've all had your turn at carrying the young lady," said he. "Why wouldn't I get her for a wee piece?"

"Ay, Jamie," replied they, pleasantly, "you may take your turn at carrying her, to be sure."

Holding his prize very tightly, he dropped down near his mother's door.

"Jamie Freel, Jamie Freel! Is that the way you treat us?" cried they, and they too dropped down near the door.

Jamie held fast, though he knew not what he was holding, for the little folk turned the lady into all sorts of strange shapes.

At one moment she was a black dog, barking and trying to bite; at another, a glowing bar of iron, which yet had no heat; then, again, a sack of wool.

But still Jamie held her, and the baffled elves were turning away, when a tiny woman, the smallest of the party, exclaimed, "Jamie Freel has her away from us, but he shall have no good o' her, for I'll make her deaf and dumb," and she threw something over the young girl.

While they rode off disappointed, Jamie lifted the latch and went in.

"Jamie, man!" cried his mother, "you've been away all night; what have they done on you?"

"Nothing bad, mother; I have the very best of good luck. Here's a beautiful young lady I have brought you

for company. "Bless us an' save us!" exclaimed the mother, and for some minutes she was so astonished that she could not think of anything else to say.

Jamie told his story of the night's adventure, ending by saying, "Surely you wouldna have allowed me to let her go with them to be lost forever?"

"But a *lady*, Jamie! How can a lady eat we'er poor diet, and live in we'er poor way? I ask you that, you foolish fellow?"

"Well, mother, sure it's better for her to be here nor over yonder," and he pointed in the direction of the castle. Meanwhile, the deaf and dumb girl shivered in her light clothing, stepping close to the humble turf fire.

"Poor creature, she's queer and handsome! No wonder they set their hearts on her," said the old woman, gazing at her guest with pity and admiration. "We must dress her first; but what, in the name o' fortune, have I fit for the likes o' her to wear?"

She went to her press in "the room," and took out her Sunday gown of brown drugget; she then opened a drawer, and drew forth a pair of white stockings, a long snowy garment of fine linen, and a cap, her "dead dress," as she called it.

These articles of attire had long been ready for a certain triste ceremony, in which she would some day fill the chief part, and only saw the light occasionally, when they were hung out to air; but she was willing to give even these to the fair trembling visitor, who was turning in dumb sorrow and wonder from her to Jamie, and from Jamie back to her.

The poor girl suffered herself to be dressed, and then sat down on a "creepie" in the chimney corner, and buried her face in her hands.

"What'll we do to keep up a lady like thou?" cried the old woman.

"I'll work for you both, mother," replied the son.

"An' how could a lady live on we'er poor diet?" she repeated.

"I'll work for her," was all Jamie's answer.

He kept his word. The young lady was very sad for a long time, and tears stole down her cheeks many an evening while the old woman spun by the fire, and Jamie made salmon nets, an accomplishment lately acquired by him, in hopes of adding to the comfort of his guest. But she was always gentle, and tried to smile when she perceived them looking at her; and by degrees she adapted herself to their ways and mode of life. It was not very long before she began to feed the pig, mash potatoes and meal for the fowls, and knit blue worsted socks.

So a year passed, and Halloween came round again. "Mother," said Jamie, taking down his cap, "I'm off to the old castle to seek my fortune."

"Are you mad, Jamie?" cried his mother, in terror, "sure they'll kill you this time for what you done on them last year." Jamie made light of her fears and went his way.

As he reached the crabtree grove, he saw bright lights in the castle windows as before, and heard loud talking. Creeping under the window, he heard the wee folk say, "That was a poor trick Jamie Freel played us this night last year, when he stole the nice young lady from us."

"Ay," said the tiny woman, "an' I punished him for it, for there she sits, a dumb image by his hearth; but he

does na' know that three drops out o' this glass I hold in my hand would give her her hearing and her speeches back again."

Jamie's heart beat fast as he entered the hall. Again he was greeted by a chorus of welcomes from the company—"Here comes Jamie Freel! Welcome, welcome, Jamie!" As soon as the tumult subsided, the little woman said, "You be to drink our health, Jamie, out o' this glass in my hand."

Jamie snatched the glass from her and darted to the door. He never knew how he reached his cabin, but he arrived there breathless, and sank on a stove by the fire.

"You're kilt surely this time, my poor boy," said his mother.

"No, indeed, better luck than ever this time!" and he gave the lady three drops of the liquid that still remained at the bottom of the glass, notwithstanding his mad race over the potato-field.

The lady began to speak, and her first words were words of thanks to Jamie.

The three inmates of the cabin had so much to say to one another, that long after cock-crow, when the fairy music had quite ceased, they were talking round the fire.

"Jamie," said the lady, "be pleased to get me paper and pen and ink, that I may write to my father, and tell him what has become of me."

She wrote, but weeks passed, and she received no answer. Again and again she wrote, and still no answer.

At length she said, "You must come with me to Dublin, Jamie, to find my father."

"I ha' no money to hire a car for you," he replied, "an' how can you travel to Dublin on your foot?"

But she implored him so much that he consented to set out with her, and walk all the way from Fannet to Dublin. It was not as easy as the fairy journey; but at last they rang the bell at the door of the house in Stephen's Green.

"Tell my father that his daughter is here," said she to the servant who opened the door.

"The gentleman that lives here has no daughter, my girl. He had one, but she died better nor a year ago."

"Do you not know me, Sullivan?"

"No, poor girl, I do not."

"Let me see the gentleman. I only ask to see him."

"Well, that's not much to ask; we'll see what can be done."

In a few moments the lady's father came to the door.

"Dear father," said she, "don't you know me?"

"How dare you call me your father?" cried the old gentleman, angrily. "You are an impostor. I have no daughter."

"Look in my face, father, and surely you'll remember me."

"My daughter is dead and buried. She died a long, long time ago." The old gentleman's voice changed from anger to sorrow. "You can go," he concluded.

"Stop, dear father, till you look at this ring on my finger. Look at your name and mine engraved on it."

"It certainly is my daughter's ring; but I do not know how you came by it. I fear in no honest way."

"Call my mother, *she* will be sure to know me," said the poor girl, who, by this time, was crying bitterly.

"My poor wife is beginning to forget her sorrow. She seldom speaks of her daughter now. Why should I renew her grief by reminding her of her loss?"

But the young lady persevered, till at last the mother was sent for.

"Mother," she began, when the old lady came to the door, "don't *you* know your daughter?"

"I have no daughter; my daughter died and was buried a long, long time ago."

"Only look in my face, and surely you'll know me."

The old lady shook her head.

"You have all forgotten me; but look at this mole on my neck. Surely, mother, you know me now?"

"Yes, yes," said the mother, "my Gracie had a mole on her neck like that; but then I saw her in her coffin, and saw the lid shut down upon her."

It became Jamie's turn to speak, and he gave the history of the fairy journey, of the theft of the young lady, of the figure he had seen laid in its place, of her life with his mother in Fannet, of last Halloween, and of the three drops that had released her from her enchantment.

She took up the story when he paused, and told how kind the mother and son had been to her.

The parents could not make enough of Jamie. They treated him with every distinction, and when he expressed his wish to return to Fannet, said they did not know what to do to show their gratitude.

But an awkward complication arose. The daughter would not let him go without her. "If Jamie goes, I'll go too," she said. "He saved me from the fairies, and has worked for me ever since. If it had not been for him, dear father and mother, you would never have seen me again. If he goes, I'll go too."

This being her resolution, the old gentleman said that Jamie should become his son-in-law. The mother was brought from Fannet in a coach and four, and there was a splendid wedding.

They all lived together in the grand Dublin house, and Jamie was heir to untold wealth at his father-in-law's death.

Forever Young

In his beautiful poem "The Stolen Child," Yeats offers the suggestion that the fairies do not steal children because they wish to torture the human parents, nor because they are of evil heart. It appears their intent is to preserve the purity and innocence of the child, to keep them in lifelong fairyhood: a world as magical as that of the child's imagination.

The Stolen Child

by William Butler Yeats

Where dips the rocky highland
Of Sleuth Wood in the lake
There lies a leafy island
Where flapping herons wake
The drowsy water-rats.

There we've hid our fairy vats
Full of berries,
And of reddest stolen cherries.
Come away, O, human child!
To the woods and waters wild,
With a fairy hand in hand,
For the world's more full of weeping than you can
understand.

Where the wave of moonlight glosses
The dim grey sands with light,
Far off by furthest Rosses
We foot it all the night,

Weaving olden dances,
Mingling hands, and mingling glances,
Till the moon has taken flight;
To and fro we leap,

And chase the frothy bubbles,
While the world is full of troubles.
And is anxious in its sleep.
Come away! O, human child!
To the woods and waters wild
With a fairy hand in hand,
For the world's more full of weeping than you can
      understand.

Where the wandering water gushes
From the hills above Glen-Car,
In pools among the rushes,
That scarce could bathe a star,
We seek for slumbering trout,
And whispering in their ears;
We give them evil dreams,
Leaning softly out

From ferns that drop their tears
Of dew on the young streams.
Come away! O, human child!
To the woods and waters wild,
With a fairy hand in hand,
For the world's more full of weeping than you can
      understand.

Away with us he's going,
The solemn-eyed:
He'll hear no more the lowing
Of the calves on the warm hillside
Or the kettle on the hob
Sing peace into his breast
Or see the brown mice bob
Round and round the oatmeal chest
For he comes, the human child,
To the waters and the wild
With a faery, hand in hand,
For the world's more full of weeping than he can
    understand.

Chapter 3
I'm Not Drunk, It's Just My Pooka
Tales of the Trickster Fairy and Its Wild Counterparts

Well, I've wrestled with reality for 35 years, Doctor, and I'm happy to state I finally won out over it.

ELWOOD P. DOWD, JIMMY STEWART'S
CHARACTER IN *HARVEY*

Not surprisingly, animals play a prominent role in the land of fairies. Whether it's their own miniature steed on which to ride across hill and dale on the blackest night, or a herd of sheep they strive to protect, the natural world from which the fairies come is the same as the place of the birds and the dragonflies, the toads and the goats. In some cases, the fairy takes the form of the animal, as is the case with the Irish *Pooka* or *Puca*, the Irish word for goblin. You'll find as many variations of spelling as the pooka itself: *Pook, Puki, Puka, Phouka, Pwca, Pwwka, Púka, Pwca,* and even *Puk* or *Puck.* The pooka can take nearly any form, including invisibility, though it is most frequently seen in the form of a horse—a black horse with eyes of fire and breath of blue flame. This horse takes the terrified mortal who is most unfortunate to have encountered it on a midnight ride that turns their hair white, but no real harm actually comes to the person . . . usually. The shapeshifter can also appear as a goat, goblin, dog, eagle, ass, and even a rabbit.

The pooka, although feared, can also be plied with gifts and in some accounts it will speak and tell one's future. Most often the pooka is encountered when one is alone on an empty lane at night, and quite often seen when one is three sheets to the wind. Because the pooka so enjoys trickery, it tends to pick on the slovenly drunkards, knowing that no one will believe the details of the outrageous encounter the next day. And though the pooka can be helpful and is most often a trickster, they can be more vicious. Pookas can turn crops, sour the milk, and make children sick. Some even believe that a pooka can cause one to commit suicide.

I drink to separate my body from my soul.

OSCAR WILDE

Douglas Hyde was a folklorist and Irish academic, preserver of the Irish language, and, in addition to being one hell of a writer, was also the first president of Ireland from 1938–1945. In Douglas Hyde's telling of *The Piper and the Puca*, we find the concept of the drunk's imagination running throughout. But who am I to judge? Certainly not the president.

The Piper and the Púca

by Douglas Hyde

In the old times there was a half fool living in Dumore, in the county Galway, and though he was excessively fond of music, he was unable to learn more than one tune, and that was the "Black Rogue." He used to get a good deal of money from the gentlemen, for they used to get sport out of him. One night the Piper was coming home from a house where there had been a dance and he was half drunk. When he came up to a little bridge that was by his mother's house, he squeezed the pipes on, and began playing the "Black Rogue." The Púca came behind him and flung him on his own back. There were long horns on the Púca, and the Piper got a good grip of them and then he said:

"Destruction on you, you nasty beast. Let me home. I have a tenpenny-piece in my pocket for my mother, and she wants snuff."

"Never mind your mother," said the Púca, "but keep your hold. If you fall, you will break your neck and your pipes." Then the Púca said to him, "Play up for me the 'Shan Van Vocht.'"

"I don't know it," said the Piper.

"Never mind whether you do or you don't," said the Púca. "Play up, and I'll make you know."

The Piper put wind in his bag, and he played such music as made himself wonder.

"Upon my word, you're a fine music-master," says the Piper, then, "but tell me where you're for bringing me."

"There's a great feast in the house of the Banshee, on the top of Croagh Patric, to-night," says the Púca, "and I'm for bringing you there to play music, and, take my word, you'll get the price of your trouble."

"By my word, you'll save me a journey, then," says the Piper, "for Father William put a journey to Croagh Patric on me because I stole the white gander from him last Martinmas."

The Púca rushed him across hills and bogs and rough places, till he brought him to the top of Croagh Patric.

Then the Púca struck three blows with his foot, and a great door opened and they passed in together into a fine room.

The Piper saw a golden table in the middle of the room, and hundreds of old women sitting round about it.

The old women rose up, and said, "A hundred thousand welcomes to you, you Púca of November. Who is this you have with you?"

"The best Piper in Ireland," says the Púca.

One of the old women struck a blow on the ground, and a door opened in the side of the wall, and what should the Piper see coming out but the white gander which he had stolen from Father William.

"By my conscience, then," says the Piper, "myself and my mother ate every taste of that gander, only one wing, and I gave that to Red Mary, and it's she told the priest I stole his gander."

The gander cleaned the table, and carried it away, and the Púca said, "Play up music for these ladies."

The Piper played up, and the old women began dancing, and they were dancing till they were tired. Then the Púca said to pay the Piper, and every old woman drew out a gold piece and gave it to him.

"By the tooth of Patric," says he, "I'm as rich as the son of a lord."

"Come with me," says the Púca, "and I'll bring you home."

They went out then, and just as he was going to ride on the Púca, the gander came up to him and gave him a new set of pipes.

The Púca was not long until he brought him to Dunmore, and he threw the Piper off at the little bridge, and then he told him to go home, and says to him, "You have two things now that you never had before—you have sense and music." The Piper went home, and he

knocked at his mother's door, saying, "Let me in, I'm as rich as a lord, and I'm the best Piper in Ireland."

"You're drunk," says the mother.

"No, indeed," says the Piper, "I haven't drunk a drop."

The mother let him in, and he gave her the gold pieces, and, "Wait now," says he, "till you hear the music I'll play."

He buckled on the pipes, but instead of music there came a sound as if all the geese and ganders in Ireland were screeching together. He wakened the neighbours, and they were all mocking him, until he put on the old pipes, and then he played melodious music for them; and after that he told them all he had gone through that night.

The next morning, when his mother went to look at the gold pieces, there was nothing there but the leaves of a plant.

The piper went to the priest and told him his story, but the priest would not believe a word from him, until he put the pipes on him, and then the screeching of the ganders and the geese began.

"Leave my sight, you thief," says the priest.

But nothing would do the Piper till he put the old pipes on him to show the priest that his story was true.

He buckled on the old pipes, and he played melodious music, and from that day till the day of his death there was never a Piper in the county Galway was as good as he was.

William's Personal Pooka

The following is from W. B. Yeats's 1888 book *Fairy and Folk Tales of the Irish Peasantry* (later republished as *Fairy and Folk Tales of Ireland*, so as not to sound so snobby). Yeats was a great scholar of Irish folklore as well as the occult. In 1911 he became a member of The Ghost Club—a paranormal research group that was one of the first of its kind! It would not surprise me to hear that Yeats himself encountered a pooka whilst roaming the country roads, warm from a pint at the pub.

The Pooka

by W. B. Yeats

The Pooka, *rectè* Púca, seems essentially an animal spirit. Some derive his name from *poc*, a he-goat; and speculative persons consider him the forefather of Shakespeare's "Puck." On solitary mountains and among old ruins he lives, "grown monstrous with much solitude," and is of the race of the nightmare. "In the MS. story, called 'Mac-na-Michomhairle,' of uncertain authorship," writes Mr. Douglas Hyde, "we read that 'out of a certain hill in Leinster, there used to emerge as far as his middle, a plump, sleek, terrible steed, and speak in human voice to each person about November-day, and he was accustomed to give intelligent and proper answers to such as consulted him concerning all that would befall them until the November of next year. And the people used to leave gifts and presents at the hill until the coming of Patrick and the holy clergy.' This tradition appears to be a cognate one with that of the Púca." Yes! Unless it were merely an *augh-ishka [each-uisgé]*, or Waterhorse. For these, we are told, were common once, and used to come out of the water to gallop on the sands and in the fields, and people would often go between them and the marge and bridle them, and they would make the finest of horses if only you could keep them away from sight of the water; but if once they saw a glimpse of the water, they would plunge in with their rider, and tear him to pieces at the bottom. It being a November spirit, however, tells in favour of the Pooka, for

November-day is sacred to the Pooka. It is hard to realise that wild, staring phantom grown sleek and civil.

He has many shapes—is now a horse, now an ass, now a bull, now a goat, now an eagle. Like all spirits, he is only half in the world of form.

Can't Someone Else Do It?

A bookseller, Patrick Kennedy was well known for his collections of folk tales of Ireland, which he gathered throughout his life (1801–1873). He is known for writing in dialect and not correcting or editing away the colloquialisms of specific areas. He is credited with helping to preserve the Irish language, including sentence structure and unique phrases. In keeping with this practice, the next story has been kept intact.

The Kildare Pooka

by Patrick Kennedy

Mr. H—— R——, when he was alive, used to live a good deal in Dublin, and he was once a great while out of the country on account of the "ninety-eight" business. But the servants kept on in the big house at Rath—all the same as if the family was at home. Well, they used to be frightened out of their lives after going to their beds with the banging of the kitchen-door, and the clattering of fire-irons, and the pots and plates and dishes. One evening they sat up ever so long, keeping one another in heart with telling stories about ghosts and fetches, and that when—what would you have of it?—the little scullery boy that used to be sleeping over the horses, and could not get room at the fire, crept into the hot hearth, and when he got tired listening to the stories, sorra fear him, but he fell dead asleep.

Well and good, after they were all gone and the kitchen fire raked up, he was woke with the noise of the kitchen door opening, and the trampling of an ass on the kitchen floor. He peeped out, and what should he see but a big ass, sure enough, sitting on his curabingo and yawning before the fire. After a little he looked about him, and began scratching his ears as if he was quite tired, and says he, "I may as well begin first as last." The poor boy's teeth began to chatter in his head, for says he, "Now he's goin' to ate me"; but the fellow with the long ears and tail on him had something else to do. He stirred the fire, and then he brought in a pail of water from the pump, and filled a big pot that he put on the fire before he went out. He then put in his hand—foot, I mean—into the hot hearth, and pulled out the little boy. He let a roar out of him with the fright, but the pooka only looked at him, and thrust out his lower lip to show how little he valued him, and then he pitched him into his pew again.

Well, he then lay down before the fire till he heard the boil coming on the water, and maybe there wasn't a plate, or a dish, or a spoon on the dresser that he didn't fetch and put into the pot, and wash and dry the whole bilin' of 'em as well as e'er a kitchen-maid from that to Dublin town. He then put all of them up on their places on the shelves; and if he didn't give a good sweepin' to the kitchen, leave it till again. Then he comes and sits foment the boy, let down one of his ears, and cocked up the other, and gave a grin. The poor fellow strove to roar out, but not a dheeg 'ud come out of his throat. The last thing the pooka done was to rake up the fire, and walk out, giving such a slap o' the door, that the boy thought the house couldn't help tumbling down.

Well, to be sure if there wasn't a hullabullo next morning when the poor fellow told his story! They could talk of nothing else the whole day. One said one thing, another said another, but a fat, lazy scullery girl said the wittiest thing of all. "Musha!" says she, "if the pooka does be cleaning up everything that way when we are asleep, what should we be slaving ourselves for doing his work?" "*Shu gu dheine*," says another, "them's the wisest words you ever said, Kauth; it's meeself won't contradict you."

So said, so done. Not a bit of a plate or dish saw a drop of water that evening, and not a besom was laid on the floor, and every one went to bed soon after sundown. Next morning everything was as fine as fine in the kitchen, and the lord mayor might eat his dinner off the flags. It was great ease to the lazy servants, you may depend, and everything went on well till a foolhardy gag of a boy said he would stay up one night and have a chat with the pooka.

He was a little daunted when the door was thrown open and the ass marched up to the fire.

"An then, sir," says he, at last, picking up courage, "if it isn't taking a liberty, might I ax who you are, and why you are so kind as to do half of the day's work for the girls every night?" "No liberty at all," says the pooka, says he: "I'll tell you, and welcome. I was a servant in the time of Squire R.'s father, and was the laziest rogue that ever was clothed and fed, and done nothing

 for it. When my time came for the other world, this is the punishment was laid on me—to come here and do all this labour every night, and then go out in the cold. It isn't so bad in the fine weather; but if you only knew what it is to stand with your head between your legs, facing the storm, from midnight to sunrise, on a bleak winter night." "And could we do anything for your comfort, my poor fellow?" says the boy. "Musha, I don't know," says the pooka, "but I think a good quilted frieze coat would help to keep the life in me them long nights." "Why then, in troth, we'd be the ungratefullest of people if we didn't feel for you."

To make a long story short, the next night but two the boy was there again; and if he didn't delight the poor pooka, holding up a fine warm coat before him, it's no mather! Betune the pooka and the man, his legs was got into the four arms of it, and it was buttoned down the breast and the belly, and he was so pleazed he walked up to the glass to see how he looked. "Well,"

says he, "it's a long lane that has no turning. I am much obliged to you and your fellow-servants. You have made me happy at last. Good-night to you."

So he was walking out, but the other cried, "Och! sure your going too soon. What about the washing and sweeping?" "Ah, you may tell the girls that they must now get their turn. My punishment was to last till I was thought worthy of a reward for the way I done my duty. You'll see me no more." And no more they did, and right sorry they were for having been in such a hurry to reward the ungrateful pooka.

What Light from Yonder Bog?

From mermaids to pookas and beyond, T. Crofton Croker's stories have that added bonus of being exquisitely written and just authentic enough to be believable. We see also a repeat appearance of the town drunk's account vs. the true story.

Daniel O'Rourke

by T. Crofton Croker

People may have heard of the renowned adventures of Daniel O'Rourke, but how few are there who know that the cause of all his perils, above and below, was neither more nor less than his having slept under the walls of the Pooka's tower. I knew the man well. He lived at the bottom of Hungry Hill, just at the right-hand side of the road as you go towards Bantry. An old man was he, at the time he told me the story, with grey hair and a red nose; and it was on the 25th of June 1813 that I heard it from his own lips, as he sat smoking his pipe under the old poplar tree, on as fine an evening as ever shone from the sky. I was going to visit the caves in Dursey Island, having spent the morning at Glengariff.

"I am often *axed* to tell it, sir," said he, "so that this is not the first time. The master's son, you see, had come from beyond foreign parts in France and Spain, as young gentlemen used to go before Buonaparte or any such was heard of; and sure enough there was a dinner given to all the people on the ground, gentle and simple, high and low, rich and poor. The *ould* gentlemen were the gentlemen after all, saving your honour's presence. They'd swear at a body a little, to be sure, and, may be, give one a cut of a whip now and then, but we were no losers by it in the end; and they were so easy and civil, and kept such rattling houses, and thousands of welcomes; and there was no grinding for rent, and there was hardly a tenant on the estate that did not taste of his landlord's bounty often and often in a year; but now it's another thing. No matter for that, sir, for I'd better be telling you my story.

"Well, we had everything of the best, and plenty of it; and we ate, and we drank, and we danced, and the young master by the same token danced with Peggy Barry, from the Bohereen—a lovely young couple they were, though they are both low enough now. To make a long story short, I got, as a body may say, the same thing as tipsy almost, for I can't remember ever at all, no ways, how it was I left the place; only I did leave it, that's certain. Well, I thought, for all that, in myself, I'd just step to Molly Cronohan's, the fairy woman, to speak a word about the bracket heifer that was bewitched; and so as I was crossing the stepping-stones of the ford of Ballyashenogh, and was looking up at the stars and blessing myself—for why? it was Lady-day—I missed my foot, and souse I fell into the water. 'Death alive!' thought I, 'I'll be drowned now!' However, I began swimming, swimming, swimming away for the dear life, till at last I got ashore, somehow or other, but never the one of me can tell how, upon a *dissolute* island.

"I wandered and wandered about there, without knowing where I wandered, until at last I got into a big bog. The moon was shining as bright as day, or your fair lady's eyes, sir (with your pardon for mentioning her), and I looked east and west, and north and south, and every way, and nothing did I see but bog, bog, bog—I could never find out how I got into it; and my heart grew cold with fear, for sure and certain I was that it would be my *berrin* place. So I sat down upon a stone which, as good luck would have it, was close by me, and I began to scratch my head, and sing the *Ullagone*— when all of a sudden the moon grew black, and I looked up, and saw something for all the world as if it was moving down between me and it, and I could not tell what it was. Down it came with a pounce, and looked at me full in the face; and what was it but an eagle? as fine a one as ever flew from the kingdom of Kerry. So he looked at me in the face, and says he to me, 'Daniel O'Rourke,' says he, 'how do you do?' 'Very well, I thank you, sir,' says I,

'I hope you're well,' wondering out of my senses all the time how an eagle came to speak like a Christian. 'What brings you here, Dan,' says he. 'Nothing at all, sir,' says I, 'only I wish I was safe home again.' 'Is it out of the island you want to go, Dan?' says he. ''Tis, sir,' says I: so I up and told him how I had taken a drop too much, and fell into the water; how I swam to the island; and how I got into the bog and did not know my way out of it. 'Dan,' says he, after a minute's thought, 'though it is very improper for you to get drunk on Lady-day, yet as you are a decent sober man, who 'tends mass well, and never fling stones at me or mine, nor cries out after us in the fields—my life for yours,' says he, 'so get up on my back, and grip me well for fear you'd fall off, and I'll fly you out of the bog.' 'I am afraid,' says I, 'your honour's making game of me; for who ever heard of riding a horseback on an eagle before?' ''Pon the honour of a gentleman,' says he, putting his right foot on his breast, 'I am quite in earnest: and so now either take my offer or starve in the bog—besides, I see that your weight is sinking the stone.'

"It was true enough as he said, for I found the stone every minute going from under me. I had no choice; so thinks I to myself, faint heart never won fair lady, and this is fair persuadance. 'I thank your honour,' says

I, 'for the loan of your civility; and I'll take your kind offer.' I therefore mounted upon the back of the eagle, and held him tight enough by the throat, and up he flew in the air like a lark. Little I knew the trick he was going to serve me. Up—up—up, God knows how far up he flew. 'Why then,' said I to him—thinking he did not know the right road home—very civilly, because why? I was in his power entirely; 'sir,' says I, 'please your honour's glory, and with humble submission to your better judgment, if you'd fly down a bit, you're now just over my cabin, and I could be put down there, and many thanks to your worship.'

"'*Arrah*, Dan,' said he, 'do you think me a fool? Look down in the next field, and don't you see two men and a gun? By my word it would be no joke to be shot this way, to oblige a drunken blackguard that I picked up off of a *could* stone in a bog.' 'Bother you,' said I to myself, but I did not speak out, for where was the use? Well, sir, up he kept, flying, flying, and I asking him every minute to fly down, and all to no use. 'Where in the world are you going, sir?' says I to him. 'Hold your tongue, Dan,' says he: 'mind your own business, and don't be interfering with the business of other people.' 'Faith, this is my business, I think,' says I. 'Be quiet, Dan,' says he: so I said no more.

"At last where should we come to, but to the moon itself. Now you can't see it from this, but there is, or there was in my time, a reaping-hook sticking out of the side of the moon, this way (drawing the figure thus ♂ on the ground with the end of his stick).

"'Dan,' said the eagle, 'I'm tired with this long fly; I had no notion 'twas so far.' 'And my lord, sir,' said I, 'who in the world *axed* you to fly so far—was it I? Did not I beg and pray and beseech you to stop half an hour ago?' 'There's no use talking, Dan,' said he, 'I'm tired bad enough, so you must get off, and sit down on the moon until I rest myself.' 'Is it sit down on the moon?' said I, 'is it upon that little round thing, then? Why, then, sure I'd fall off in a minute, and be *kilt* and spilt, and smashed all to bits; you are a vile deceiver—so you are.' 'Not at all, Dan,' said he, 'you can catch fast hold of the reaping-hook that's sticking out of the side of the moon, and 'twill keep you up.' 'I won't then,' said I. 'May be not,' said he, quite quiet. 'If you don't, my man, I shall just give you a shake, and one slap of my wing, and send you down to the ground, where every bone in your body will be smashed as small as a drop of dew on a cabbage-leaf in the morning.' 'Why, then, I'm in a fine way,' said I to myself, 'ever to have come along with the likes of you.' And so giving him a hearty curse in Irish, for fear he'd know what I said, I got off his back with a heavy heart, took hold of the reaping-hook, and sat down upon the moon, and a mighty cold seat it was, I can tell you that.

"When he had me there fairly landed, he turned about on me, and said, 'Good morning to you, Daniel O'Rourke,' said he; 'I think I've nicked you fairly now. You robbed my nest last year' ('twas true enough for him, but how he found it out is hard to say), 'and in return you are freely welcome to cool your heels dangling upon the moon like a cockthrow.'

"'Is that all, and is this the way you leave me, you brute, you,' says I. 'You ugly unnatural *baste*, and is this the way you serve me at last? Bad luck to yourself, with your hook'd nose, and to all your breed, you blackguard.' 'Twas all to no manner of use; he spread out his great big wings, burst out a laughing, and flew away like lightning. I bawled after him to stop; but I might have called and bawled for ever, without his minding me. Away he went, and I never saw him from that day to this—sorrow fly away with him! You may be sure I was in a disconsolate condition, and kept roaring out for the bare grief, when all at once a door opened right in the middle of the moon, creaking on its hinges as if it had not been opened for a month before, I suppose they never thought of greasing 'em, and out there walks— who do you think, but the man in the moon himself? I knew him by his bush.

"'Good morrow to you, Daniel O'Rourke,' said he, 'how do you do?' 'Very well, thank your honour,' said I. 'I hope your honour's well.' 'What brought you here, Dan?' said he. So I told him how I was a little overtaken in liquor at the master's, and how I was cast on a dissolute island, and how I lost my way in the bog, and how the thief of an eagle promised to fly me out of it, and how, instead of that, he had fled me up to the moon.

"'Dan,' said the man in the moon, taking a pinch of snuff when I was done, 'you must not stay here.' 'Indeed, sir,' says I, ''tis much against my will I'm here at all; but how am I to go back?' 'That's your business,' said he, 'Dan, mine is to tell you that here you must not stay; so be off in less than no time.' 'I'm doing no harm,' says I, 'only holding on hard by the reaping-hook, lest I fall off.' 'That's what you must not do, Dan,' says he. 'Pray, sir,' says I, 'may I ask how many you are in family, that you would not give a poor traveller lodging: I'm sure 'tis not so often you're troubled with strangers coming to see you, for 'tis a long way.' 'I'm by myself,

Dan,' says he, 'but you'd better let go the reaping-hook.' 'Faith, and with your leave,' says I, 'I'll not let go the grip, and the more you bids me, the more I won't let go—so I will.' 'You had better, Dan,' says he again. 'Why, then, my little fellow,' says I, taking the whole weight of him with my eye from head to foot, 'there are two words to that bargain; and I'll not budge, but you may if you like.' 'We'll see how that is to be,' says he, and back he went, giving the door such a great bang after him (for it was plain he was huffed) that I thought the moon and all would fall down with it.

"Well, I was preparing myself to try strength with him, when back again he comes, with the kitchen cleaver in his hand, and, without saying a word, he gives two bangs to the handle of the reaping-hook that was keeping me up, and *whap!* it came in two. 'Good morning to you, Dan,' says the spiteful little old blackguard, when he saw me cleanly falling down with a bit of the handle in my hand. 'I thank you for your visit, and fair weather after you, Daniel.' I had not time to make any answer to him, for I was tumbling over and over, and rolling and rolling, at the rate of a fox-hunt. 'God help me!' says I, 'but this is a pretty pickle for a decent man to be seen in at this time of night: I am now sold fairly.' The word was not out of my mouth when, whiz! what should fly by close to my ear but a flock of wild geese, all the way from my own bog of Ballyasheenogh, else how should they know *me*? The *ould* gander, who was their general, turning about his head, cried out to me, 'Is that you, Dan?' 'The same,' said I, not a bit daunted now at what he said, for I was by this time used to all kinds of *bedevilment*, and, besides, I knew him of *ould*. 'Good morrow to you,' says he, 'Daniel O'Rourke; how are you in health this morning?' 'Very well, sir,' says I, 'I thank you kindly,' drawing my breath, for I was mightily in want of some. 'I hope your honour's the same.' 'I think 'tis falling you are, Daniel,' says he. 'You may say that, sir,' says I. 'And where are you going all the way so fast?' said the gander. So I told him how I had taken the drop, and how I came on the island, and how I lost my way in the bog, and how the thief of an eagle flew me up to the moon, and how the man in the moon turned me out. 'Dan,' said he, 'I'll save you: put out your hand and catch me by the leg, and I'll fly you home.' 'Sweet is your hand in a pitcher of honey, my jewel,' says I, though all the time I thought within myself that I don't much trust you; but there was no help, so I caught the gander by the leg, and away I and the other geese flew after him as fast as hops.

"We flew, and we flew, and we flew, until we came right over the wide ocean. I knew it well, for I saw Cape Clear to my right hand, sticking up out of the water. 'Ah, my lord,' said I to the goose, for I thought it best to keep a civil tongue in my head any way, 'fly to land if you please.' 'It is impossible, you see, Dan,' said he, 'for a while, because you see we are going to Arabia.' 'To Arabia!' said I, 'that's surely some place in foreign parts, far away. Oh! Mr. Goose: why then, to be sure, I'm a man to be pitied among you.' 'Whist, whist, you fool,' said he, 'hold your tongue; I tell you Arabia is a very decent sort of place, as like West Carbery as one egg is like another, only there is a little more sand there.'

"Just as we were talking, a ship hove in sight, scudding so beautiful before the wind. 'Ah! then, sir,' said I, 'will you drop me on the ship, if you please?' 'We are not fair over it,' said he. 'If I dropped you now you would go splash into the sea.' 'I would not,' says I. 'I

know better than that, for it is just clean under us, so let me drop now at once.'

"'If you must, you must,' said he. 'There, take your own way,' and he opened his claw, and faith he was right—sure enough I came down plump into the very bottom of the salt sea! Down to the very bottom I went, and I gave myself up then for ever, when a whale walked up to me, scratching himself after his night's sleep, and looked me full in the face, and never the word did he say, but lifting up his tail, he splashed me all over again with the cold salt water till there wasn't a dry stitch upon my whole carcass! and I heard somebody saying—'twas a voice I knew, too—'Get up, you drunken brute, off o' that,' and with that I woke up, and there was Judy with a tub full of water, which she was splashing all over me—for, rest her soul! though she was a good wife, she never could bear to see me in drink, and had a bitter hand of her own.

"'Get up,' said she again: 'and of all places in the parish would no place *sarve* your turn to lie down upon but under the *ould* walls of Carrigapooka? uneasy resting I am sure you had of it.' And sure enough I had: for I was fairly bothered out of my senses with eagles,

and men of the moons, and flying ganders, and whales, driving me through bogs, and up to the moon, and down to the bottom of the green ocean. If I was in drink ten times over, long would it be before I'd lie down in the same spot again, I know that."

Unbridled Passion

Along with his singular collection on leprechauns, D. R. McAnally knows a thing or two about pookas and how to get the best of them. It's a fitting, and perhaps mildly comforting end to a chapter of trickery and wild rides, to know that there is actually a glimmer of hope for all ye who wander those roads at night, stumbling across a stone (or was that just the last pint taking hold?).

Taming the Pooka

by D. R. McAnally

The west and northwest coast of Ireland shows many remarkable geological formations, but, excepting the Giant's Causeway, no more striking spectacle is presented than that to the south of Galway Bay. From the sea, the mountains rise in terraces like gigantic stairs, the layers of stone being apparently harder and denser on the upper surfaces than beneath, so the lower portion of each layer, disintegrating first, is washed away by the rains and a clearly defined step is formed. These terraces are generally about twenty feet high, and of a breadth, varying with the situation and exposure, of from ten to fifty feet.

The highway from Ennis to Ballyvaughn, a fishing village opposite Galway, winds, by a circuitous course, through these freaks of nature, and, on the long descent from the high land to the sea level, passes the most conspicuous of the neighboring mountains, the Corkscrew Hill. The general shape of the mountain is conical, the terraces composing it are of wonderful regularity from the base to the peak, and the strata being sharply upturned from the horizontal, the impression given is that of a broad road carved out of the sides of the mountain and winding by an easy ascent to the summit.

"'Tis the Pooka's Path they call it," said the car-man. "Phat's the Pooka? Well, that's not aisy to say. It's an avil sper't that does be always in mischief, but sure it niver does sarious harrum axceptin' to thim that desarves it, or thim that shpakes av it disrespictful. I never seen it, Glory be to God, but there's thim that has, and be the same token, they do say that it looks like the finest black horse that iver wore shoes. But it isn't a horse at all at all, for no horse 'ud have eyes av fire, or be breathin' flames av blue wid a shmell o' sulfur, savin' yer presince, or a shnort like thunder, and no mortial horse 'ud take the lapes it does, or go as fur widout gettin' tired. Sure when it give Tim O'Bryan the ride it give him, it wint from Gort to Athlone wid wan jump, an' the next it tuk he was in Mullingyar, and the next was in Dublin, and

back agin be way av Kilkenny an' Limerick, an' niver turned a hair. How far is that? Faith I dunno, but it's a power av distance, an' clane acrost Ireland an' back. He knew it was the Pooka bekase it shpake to him like a Christian mortial, only it isn't agrayble in its language an' 'ull niver give ye a dacint word afther ye're on its back, an' sometimes not before aither.

"Sure Dennis O'Rourke was afther comin' home wan night, it was only a boy I was, but I mind him tellin' the shtory, an' it was at a fair in Galway he'd been. He'd been havin' a sup, some says more, but whin he come to the rath, and jist beyant where the fairies dance and ferninst the wall where the polisman was shot last winther, he fell in the ditch, quite spint and tired complately. It wasn't the length as much as the wideness av the road was in it, fur he was goin' from wan side to the other an' it was too much fur him entirely. So he laid shtill fur a bit and thin thried fur to get up, but his legs wor light and his head was heavy, an' whin he attempted to get his feet an the road 'twas his head that was an it, bekase his legs cudn't balance it. Well, he laid there and was bet entirely, an' while he was studyin' how he'd raise, he heard the throttin' av a horse on the road. ''Tis meself 'ull get the lift now,' says he, and laid waitin', and up comes the Pooka. Whin

Dennis seen him, begob, he kivered his face wid his hands and turned on the breast av him, and roared wid fright like a bull.

'Arrah thin, ye snakin' blaggârd,' says the Pooka, mighty short, 'lave aff yer bawlin' or I'll kick ye to the ind av next week,' says he to him.

"'Arrah thin, ye snakin' blaggârd,' says the Pooka, mighty short, 'lave aff yer bawlin' or I'll kick ye to the ind av next week,' says he to him.

"But Dennis was scairt, an' bellered louder than afore, so the Pooka, wid his hoof, give him a crack on the back that knocked the wind out av him.

"'Will ye lave aff,' says the Pooka, 'or will I give ye another, ye roarin' dough-face?'

"Dennis left aff blubberin' so the Pooka got his timper back.

"'Shtand up, ye guzzlin' sarpint,' says the Pooka, 'I'll give ye a ride.'

"'Plaze yer Honor,' says Dennis, 'I can't. Sure I've not been afther drinkin' at all, but shmokin' too much an' atin', an' it's sick I am, and not ontoxicated.'

"'Och, ye dhrunken buzzard,' says the Pooka, 'Don't offer fur to desave me,' liftin' up his hoof agin, an' givin' his tail a swish that sounded like the noise av a catheract, 'Didn't I thrack ye for two miles be yer breath,' says he, 'An' you shmellin' like a potheen fact'ry,' says he, 'An' the nose on yer face as red as a turkey-cock's. Get up, or I'll lift ye,' says he, jumpin' up an' cracking his hind fut like he was doin' a jig.

"Dennis did his best, an' the Pooka helped him wid a grip o' the teeth on his collar.

"'Pick up yer caubeen,' says the Pooka, 'an' climb up. I'll give ye such a ride as ye niver dhramed av.'

"'Ef it's plazin' to yer Honor,' says Dennis, 'I'd laver walk. Ridin' makes me dizzy,' says he.

"''Tis not plazin',' says the Pooka, 'will ye get up or will I kick the shtuffin' out av yer cowardly carkidge,' says he, turnin' round an' flourishin' his heels in Dennis' face.

"Poor Dennis thried, but he cudn't, so the Pooka tuk him to the wall an' give him a lift an it, an' whin Dennis was mounted, an' had a tight howld on the mane, the first lep he give was down the rock there, a

thousand feet into the field ye see, thin up agin, an' over the mountain, an' into the say, an' out agin, from the top av the waves to the top av the mountain, an' afther the poor soggarth av a ditcher was nigh onto dead, the Pooka come back here wid him an' dhropped him in the ditch where he found him, an' blowed in his face to put him to slape, so lavin' him. An' they found Dennis in the mornin' an' carried him home, no more cud he walk for a fortnight be razon av the wakeness av his bones fur the ride he'd had.

"But sure, the Pooka's a different baste entirely to phat he was afore King Bryan-Boru tamed him. Niver heard av him? Well, he was the king av Munster an' all Ireland an' tamed the Pooka wanst fur all on the Corkschrew Hill ferninst ye.

"Ye see, in the owld days, the counthry was full av avil sper'ts, an' fairies an' witches, an' divils entirely, and the harrum they done was onsaycin', for they wor always comin' an' goin', like Mulligan's blanket, an' widout so much as sayin', by yer lave. The fairies 'ud be dancin' on the grass every night be the light av the moon, an' stalin' away the childhre, an' many's the wan they tuk that niver come back. The owld rath on the hill beyant was full av the dead, an' afther nightfall they'd come from their graves an' walk in a long line wan afther another to the owld church in the valley where they'd go in an' stay till cock-crow, thin they'd come out agin an' back to the rath. Sorra a parish widout a witch, an' some nights they'd have a great enthertainmint on the Corkschrew Hill, an' you'd see thin wid shnakes on their arrums an' necks an' ears, be way av jewels, an' the eyes av dead men in their hair, comin' for miles an' miles, some ridin' through the air on shticks an' bats an' owls, an' some walkin', an' more on Pookas an' horses wid wings that 'ud come up in line to the top av the hill, like the cabs at the dure o' the theayter, an' lave thim there an' hurry aff to bring more.

"Sometimes the Owld Inimy, Satan himself, 'ud be there at the enthertainmint, comin' an a monsthrous draggin, wid grane shcales an' eyes like the lightnin' in the heavens, an' a roarin' fiery mouth like a lime-kiln. It was the great day thin, for they do say all the witches brought their ray-ports at thim saysons fur to show him phat they done.

"Some 'ud tell how they shtopped the wather in a spring, an' inconvanienced the nabers, more 'ud show

how they dhried the cow's milk, an' made her kick the pail, an' they'd all laugh like to shplit. Some had blighted the corn, more had brought the rains on the harvest. Some towld how their enchantmints made the childhre fall ill, some said how they set the thatch on fire, more towld how they shtole the eggs, or spiled the crame in the churn, or bewitched the butther so it 'udn't come, or led the shape into the bog. But that wasn't all.

"Wan 'ud have the head av a man murthered be her manes, an' wid it the hand av him hung fur the murther; wan 'ud bring the knife she'd scuttled a boat wid an' pint in the say to where the corpses laid av the fishermen she'd dhrownded; wan 'ud carry on her breast the child she'd shtolen an' meant to bring up in avil, an' another wan 'ud show the little white body av a babby she'd smothered in its slape. And the corpse-candles

'ud tell how they desaved the thraveller, bringin' him to the river, an' the avil sper'ts 'ud say how they dhrew him in an' down to the bottom in his sins an' thin to the pit wid him. An' owld Belzebub 'ud listen to all av thim, wid a rayporther, like thim that's afther takin' down the spaches at a Lague meetin', be his side, a-writing phat they said, so as whin they come to be paid, it 'udn't be forgotten.

"Thim wor the times fur the Pookas too, fur they had power over thim that wint forth afther night, axceptin' it was on an arriant av marcy they were. But sorra a sinner that hadn't been to his juty reglar 'ud iver see the light av day agin afther meetin' a Pooka thin, for the baste 'ud aither kick him to shmithereens where he stud, or lift him on his back wid his teeth an' jump into the say wid him, thin dive, lavin' him to dhrownd, or shpring over a clift wid him an' tumble him to the bottom a bleedin' corpse. But wasn't there the howls av joy whin a Pooka 'ud catch a sinner unbeknownst, an' fetch him on the Corkschrew wan o' the nights Satan was there. Och, God defind us, phat a sight it was. They made a ring wid the corpse-candles, while the witches tore him limb from limb, an' the fiends drunk his blood in red-hot iron noggins wid shrieks o' laughter to smother his schreams, an' the Pookas jumped on his

body an' thrampled it into the ground, an' the timpest 'ud whishle a chune, an' the mountains about 'ud kape time, an' the Pookas, an' witches, an' sper'ts av avil, an' corpse-candles, an' bodies o' the dead, an' divils, 'ud all jig together round the rock where owld Belzebub 'ud set shmilin', as fur to say he'd ax no betther divarshun. God's presince be wid us, it makes me crape to think av it.

"Well, as I was afther sayin', in the time av King Bryan, the Pookas done a dale o' harrum, but as thim that they murthered wor dhrunken bastes that wor in the shebeens in the day an' in the ditch be night, an' wasn't missed whin the Pookas tuk them, the King paid no attintion, an' small blame to him that 's.

"But wan night, the queen's babby fell ill, an' the king says to his man, says he, 'Here, Riley, get you up an' on the white mare an' go fur the docther.'

"'Musha thin,' says Riley, an' the king's counthry house was in the break o' the hills, so Riley 'ud pass the rath an' the Corkschrew on the way afther the docther; 'Musha thin,' says he, aisey and on the quiet, 'it's mesilf that doesn't want that same job.'

"So he says to the king, 'Won't it do in the mornin'?'

"'It will not,' says the king to him. 'Up, ye lazy beggar, atin' me bread, an' the life lavin' me child.'

"So he wint, wid great shlowness, tuk the white mare, an' aff, an' that was the last seen o' him or the mare aither, fur the Pooka tuk 'em. Sorra a taste av a lie's in it, for thim that said they seen him in Cork two days afther, thrading aff the white mare, was desaved be the sper'ts, that made it seem to be him whin it wasn't that they've a thrick o' doin'.

"Well, the babby got well agin, bekase the docther didn't get there, so the king left botherin' afther it and begun to wondher about Riley an' the white mare, and sarched fur thim but didn't find thim. An' thin he knewn that they was gone entirely, bekase, ye see, the Pooka didn't lave as much as a hair o' the mare's tail.

"'Wurra thin,' says he, 'is it horses that the Pooka 'ull be stalin'? Bad cess to its impidince! This 'ull niver do. Sure we'll be ruinated entirely,' says he.

"Mind ye now, it's my consate from phat he said, that the king wasn't consarned much about Riley, fur he knewn that he cud get more Irishmen whin he wanted thim, but phat he meant to say was that if the Pooka tuk to horse-stalin', he'd be ruin-ated entirely, so he would, for where 'ud he get another white mare? So it was a mighty sarious question an' he retired widin himself in the coort wid a big book that he had that towld saycrets. He'd a sight av larnin', had the king, aquel to a school-masther, an' a head that 'ud sarcumvint a fox.

"So he read an' read as fast as he cud, an' afther readin' widout shtoppin', barrin' fur the bit an' sup, fur siven days an' nights, he come out, an' whin they axed him cud he bate the Pooka now, he said niver a word, axceptin' a wink wid his eye, as fur to say he had him.

"So that day he was in the fields an' along be the hedges an' ditches from sunrise to sunset, collectin' the matarials av a dose fur the Pooka, but phat he got, faith, I dunno, no more does any wan, fur he never said, but kep the saycret to himself an' didn't say it aven to the quane, fur he knewn that saycrets run through a woman like wather in a ditch. But there was wan thing about it that he cudn't help tellin', fur he wanted it but cudn't get it widout help, an' that was three hairs from the Pooka's tail, axceptin' which the charm 'udn't work. So he towld a man he had, he'd give him no end av goold if he'd get thim fur him, but the felly pulled aff his caubeen an' scrotched his head an' says, 'Faix, yer Honor, I dunno phat'll be the good to me av the goold if the Pooka gets a crack at me carkidge wid his hind heels,' an' he wudn't undhertake the job on no wages, so the king begun to be afeared that his loaf was dough.

"But it happen'd av the Friday, this bein' av a Chewsday, that the Pooka caught a sailor that hadn't been on land only long enough to get bilin' dhrunk, an' got him on his back, so jumped over the clift wid him lavin' him dead enough, I go bail. Whin they come to sarch the sailor to see phat he had in his pockets, they found three long hairs round the third button av his top-coat. So they tuk thim to the king tellin' him where they got thim, an' he was greatly rejiced, bekase now he belaved he had the Pooka sure enough, so he ended his inchantmint.

"But as the avenin' come, he riz a doubt in the mind av him thish-a-way. Ev the three hairs wor out av the Pooka's tail, the charm 'ud be good enough, but if they wasn't, an' was from his mane inshtead, or from a horse inshtead av a Pooka, the charm 'udn't work an' the Pooka 'ud get atop av him wid all the feet he had at wanst an' be the death av him immejitly. So this nate and outprobrious argymint shtruck the king wid great force an' fur a bit, he was onaisey. But wid a little sarcumvintion, he got round it, for he confist an' had absolution so as he'd be ready, thin he towld wan av the sarvints to come in an' tell him afther supper, that there was a poor widdy in the boreen beyant the Corkschrew that wanted help that night, that it 'ud be an arriant av marcy he'd be on, an' so safe agin the Pooka if the charm didn't howld.

"'Sure, phat'll be the good o' that?' says the man, 'It 'ull be a lie, an' won't work.'

"'Do you be aisey in yer mind,' says the king to him agin, 'do as yer towld an' don't argy, for that's a pint av mettyfisics,' says he, faix it was a dale av deep larnin' he had, 'that's a pint av mettyfisics an' the more ye argy on thim subjics, the less ye know,' says he, an' it's thrue fur him. 'Besides, aven if it's a lie, it'll desave the Pooka, that's no mettyfishian, an' it's my belafe that the end is good enough for the manes,' says he, a-thinking av the white mare.

"So, afther supper, as the king was settin' afore the fire, an' had the charm in his pocket, the sarvint come in and towld him about the widdy.

"'Begob,' says the king, like he was surprised, so as to desave the Pooka complately, 'Ev that's thrue, I must go relave her at wanst.' So he riz an' put on sojer boots, wid shpurs on 'em a fut acrost, an' tuk a long whip in his hand, for fear, he said, the widdy 'ud have dogs, thin wint to his chist an' tuk his owld stockin' an' got a suv'rin out av it—Och, 'twas the shly wan he was, to do everything so well—an' wint out wid his right fut first, an' the shpurs a-rattlin' as he walked.

"He come acrost the yard, an' up the hill beyant yon an' round the corner, but seen nothin' at all. Thin up the fut path round the Corkscrew an' met niver a sowl but a dog that he cast a shtone at. But he didn't go out av the road to the widdy's, for he was afeared that if he met the Pooka an' he caught him in a lie, not bein' in the road to where he said he was goin', it 'ud be all over wid him. So he walked up an' down bechuxt the owld church below there an' the rath on the hill, an' jist as the clock was shtrikin' fur twelve, he heard a horse in front av him, as he was walkin' down, so he turned an' wint the other way, gettin' his charm ready, an' the Pooka come up afther him.

"'The top o' the mornin' to yer Honor,' says the Pooka, as perlite as a Frinchman, for he seen be his close that the king wasn't a common blaggârd like us, but was wan o' the rale quolity.

"'Me sarvice to ye,' says the king to him agin, as bowld as a ram, an' whin the Pooka heard him shpake, he got perliter than iver, an' made a low bow an' shcrape wid his fut, thin they wint on together an' fell into discoorse.

"''Tis a black night for thravelin',' says the Pooka.

"'Indade it is,' says the king, 'it's not me that 'ud be out in it, if it wasn't a case o' needcessity. I'm on an arriant av charity,' says he.

"'That's rale good o' ye,' says the Pooka to him, 'and if I may make bowld to ax, phat's the needcessity?'

"''Tis to relave a widdy-woman,' says the king.

"'Oho,' says the Pooka, a-throwin' back his head laughin' wid great plazin'ness an' nudgin' the king wid his leg on the arrum, beways that it was a joke it was bekase the king said it was to relave a widdy he was goin'. 'Oho,' says the Pooka, ''tis mesilf that's glad to be in the comp'ny av an iligint jintleman that's on so plazin' an arriant av marcy,' says he. 'An' how owld is the widdy-woman?' says he, bustin' wid the horrid laugh he had.

"'Musha thin,' says the king, gettin' red in the face an' not likin' the joke the laste bit, for jist betune us, they do say that afore he married the quane, he was the laddy-buck wid the wimmin, an' the quane's maid towld the cook, that towld the footman, that said to the gârdener, that towld the nabers that many's the night the poor king was as wide awake as a hare from sun to sun wid the quane a-gostherin' at him about that same. More betoken, there was a widdy in it, that was as sharp as a rat-thrap an' surrounded him whin he was young an' hadn't as much sinse as a goose, an' was like to marry him at wanst in shpite av all his relations, as widdys undhershtand how to do. So it's my consate that it wasn't dacint for the Pooka to be afther laughin' that-a-way, an' shows that avil sper'ts is dirthy blaggârds that can't talk wid jintlemin. 'Musha,' thin, says the king, bekase the Pooka's laughin' wasn't agrayble to listen to, 'I don't know that same, fur I niver seen her, but, be jagers, I belave she's a hundherd, an' as ugly as Belzebub, an' whin her owld man was alive, they tell me she had a timper like a gandher, an' was as aisey to manage as an armful o' cats,' says he. 'But she's in want, an' I'm afther bringin' her a suv'rin,' says he.

"Well, the Pooka sayced his laughin', fur he seen the king was very vexed, an' says to him, 'And if it's plazin', where does she live?'

"'At the ind o' the boreen beyant the Corkschrew,' says the king, very short.

"'Begob, that's a good bit,' says the Pooka.

"'Faix, it's thrue for ye,' says the king, 'more betoken, it's up hill ivery fut o' the way, an' me back is bruk entirely wid the stapeness,' says he, be way av a hint he'd like a ride.

"'Will yer Honor get upon me back,' says the Pooka. 'Sure I'm afther goin' that-a-way, an' you don't mind gettin' a lift?' says he, a-fallin' like the stupid baste he was, into the thrap the king had made fur him.

"'Thanks,' says the king, 'I b'lave not. I've no bridle nor saddle,' says he, 'besides, it's the shpring o' the year, an' I'm afeared ye're sheddin', an' yer hair 'ull come aff an' spile me new britches,' says he, lettin' on to make axcuse.

"'Have no fear,' says the Pooka. 'Sure I niver drop me hair. It's no ordhinary garron av a horse I am, but a most oncommon baste that's used to the quolity,' says he.

"'Yer spache shows that,' says the king, the clever man that he was, to be perlite that-a-way to a Pooka, that's known to be a divil out-en-out, 'but ye must exqueeze me this avenin', bekase, d'ye mind, the road's full o' shtones an' monsthrous stape, an' ye look so young, I'm afeared ye'll shtumble an' give me a fall,' says he.

"'Arrah thin,' says the Pooka, 'it's thrue fur yer Honor, I do look young,' an' he begun to prance on the road givin' himself airs like an owld widdy man afther wantin' a young woman, 'but me age is owlder than ye'd suppoge. How owld 'ud ye say I was,' says he, shmilin'.

"'Begorra, divil a bit know I,' says the king, 'but if it's agrayble to ye, I'll look in yer mouth an' give ye an answer,' says he.

"So the Pooka come up to him fair an' soft an' stratched his mouth like as he thought the king was wantin' fur to climb in, an' the king put his hand on his jaw like as he was goin' to see the teeth he had: and thin, that minnit he shlipped the three hairs round the Pooka's jaw, an' whin he done that, he dhrew thim tight, an' said the charm crossin' himself the while, an' immejitly the hairs wor cords av stale, an' held the Pooka tight, be way av a bridle.

"'Arra-a-a-h, now, ye bloody baste av a murtherin' divil ye,' says the king, pullin' out his big whip that he had consaled in his top-coat, an' giving the Pooka a crack wid it undher his stummick, 'I'll give ye a ride ye won't forgit in a hurry,' says he, 'ye black Turk av a four-legged nagur an' you shtaling me white mare,' says he, hittin' him agin.

"'Oh my,' says the Pooka, as he felt the grip av the iron on his jaw an' knewn he was undher an inchantmint, 'Oh my, phat's this at all,' rubbin' his breast wid his hind heel, where the whip had hit him, an' thin jumpin' wid his fore feet out to cotch the air an' thryin' fur to break away. 'Sure I'm ruined, I am, so I am,' says he.

"'It's thrue fur ye,' says the king, 'begob it's the wan thrue thing ye iver said,' says he, a-jumpin' on his back, an' givin' him the whip an' the two shpurs wid all his might.

"Now I forgot to tell ye that whin the king made his inchantmint, it was good fur siven miles round, and the Pooka knewn that same as well as the king an' so he shtarted like a cunshtable was afther him, but the king was afeared to let him go far, thinkin' he'd do the siven miles in a jiffy, an' the inchantmint 'ud be broken like a rotten shtring, so he turned him up the Corkschrew.

"'I'll give ye all the axercise ye want,' says he, 'in thravellin' round this hill,' an' round an' round they wint, the king shtickin' the big shpurs in him every jump an' crackin' him wid the whip till his sides run blood in shtrames like a mill race, an' his schreams av pain wor heard all over the worruld so that the king av France opened his windy and axed the polisman why he didn't shtop the fightin' in the shtrate. Round an' round an' about the Corkschrew wint the king, a-lashin' the Pooka, till his feet made the path ye see on the hill bekase he wint so often.

"And whin mornin' come, the Pooka axed the king phat he'd let him go fur, an' the king was gettin' tired an' towld him that he must niver shtale another horse, an' never kill another man, barrin' furrin blaggârds that wasn't Irish, an' whin he give a man a ride, he must bring him back to the shpot where he got him an' lave him there. So the Pooka consinted, Glory be to God, an' got aff, an' that's the way he was tamed, an' axplains how it was that Dennis O'Rourke was left be the Pooka in the ditch jist where he found him."

"More betoken, the Pooka's an althered baste every way, fur now he dhrops his hair like a common horse, and it's often found shtickin' to the hedges where he jumped over, an' they do say he doesn't shmell half as shtrong o' sulfur as he used, nor the fire out o' his nose isn't so bright. But all the king did fur him 'ud n't taiche him to be civil in his spache, an' whin he meets ye in the way, he spakes just as much like a blaggârd as ever. An' it's out av divilmint entirely he does it, bekase he can be perlite as ye know be phat I towld ye av him sayin' to the king, an' that proves phat I said to ye that avil sper'ts can't larn rale good manners, no matther how hard they thry.

"But the fright he got never left him, an' so he kapes out av the highways an' thravels be the futpaths, an' so isn't often seen. An' it's my belafe that he can do no harrum at all to thim that fears God, an' there's thim that says he niver shows himself nor meddles wid man nor mortial barrin' they're in dhrink, an' mebbe there's something in that too, fur it doesn't take much dhrink to make a man see a good dale."

The problem with the world is that everyone is a few drinks behind.

HUMPHREY BOGART

Chapter 4
Is That All There Is?
Fairies Who Give, or the Barter System

A moment after the fairy's entrance the window was blown open by the breathing of the little stars, and Peter dropped in. He had carried Tinker Bell part of the way, and his hand was still messy with the fairy dust.

"Tinker Bell," he called softly, after making sure that the children were asleep, "Tink, where are you?" She was in a jug for the moment, and liking it extremely; she had never been in a jug before.

"Oh, do come out of that jug, and tell me, do you know where they put my shadow?"

The loveliest tinkle as of golden bells answered him. It is the fairy language. You ordinary children

can never hear it, but if you were to hear it you
would know that you had heard it once before.

J. M. BARRIE, *PETER PAN*

And now we come to the kinder, gentler portion of the book (secretly hidden here, so that you are good and scared and deserving of a bit of a break from all that wickedness). The truth is, fairies can be solicited for help, but most often they offer a reward to someone whose act of kindness sets them apart from their fellow man. A young woman pours the cleanest draught of water for a wayside hag, a sweet little girl is orphaned and left with hardly a thing to remind her of her parents.

Here is when fairies step in, reward the bravest acts and purest of hearts.

Here is when fairies step in, reward the bravest acts and purest of hearts.

It is said that fairies, if they like you, will take pity on you if you are lost in the woods and help guide you out. As with house brownies and some hobgoblins, fairies are always willing to pitch in, provided that you treat them with kindness and respect (and fill their cups each night). The modern idea of fairy tales, where goodness is rewarded, is a necessary contrast to the snarling, devilish, trickster world of the pooka, leprechaun, and goblin. It is, perhaps, what keeps us coming back for more. The fairy godmothers await the critical moment to bestow salvation.

This next story, written by contemporary author, storyteller, and keeper of the fairy ways, Dolores Guetebier, holds all the classical elements of a wish-granting fairy tale. Note the confusion that the little girl feels in the otherwise familiar forest, where she is made dizzy with the smells and sounds of the forest. This is a sure sign of fairy enchantment: it is not unlike the poor fool who happens upon a fairy party and joins in the dance, just to discover that years have passed when he wakes up from the enchanted soiree. In this story, however, we are reminded of the pure heart of a child who has suffered so much loss, who does not ask for riches, and who is chosen by the fae folk to be worthy. These attributes are impossible to fake: fairies are keen observers of both actions and feelings. When they do encounter the rare human who is truly deserving of having their wishes come true, fairies do protect and grant, rather than lure and trick. It is also important to point out that though the child is not seeking the help of the fairies, her ability to accept and believe them as real is also rewarded. This harkens back to the poem of W. B. Yeats that gives claim that fairies only steal children that they wish to protect from the ugliness of the world.

The Magic Teacup

by Dolores Guetebier

Once upon a time—long, long ago—deep in the Black Forest of Germany, there lived a little girl named Dora. She lived with her mother and father. They were very happy until, one day, her father was killed when he fell while climbing a very high mountain to pick Dora some edelweiss. Soon after, her mother died when the old cow—Gertrude—rolled over on her.

Little Dora was ten when she went to live with her Auntie Bruna at the other edge of the Black Forest. Auntie Bruna gave Dora a little teacup and saucer that had been Dora's mother's, and her mother's mother's, and her mother's mother's mother's.

"It used to belong to your Great, Great Grandmother Theodora," Aunt Bruna explained. "There was a whole set, but over the years the pieces have been broken. This one cup and saucer are all that are left. Grandma Theodora said they were magical, a gift from the fairies. Many, many years ago your mother asked me to save them and give them to you, if anything should happen to her." Aunt Bruna smiled as she gave Dora the cup and saucer.

"Oh, it is beautiful!" exclaimed Dora. They were very beautiful indeed. They were made of a glass that shone like opals, and around the edge of the cup a vine curved and twisted throughout a beautiful handle so delicate, and yet strong, so like her beloved Black Forest. The saucer's edge was entwined with the same delicate wreath. How Dora loved them!

One day Aunt Bruna sent little Dora into the woods to pick some white, star-shaped flowers called Nightshade for the herb shelf, as well as a basket of mushrooms to add to the soup Bruna was preparing for supper.

Dora followed a path Aunt Bruna had taken her on many times, but somehow she took a wrong turn and wandered deeper and deeper into the forest. She became enchanted with the many wildflowers, the beautiful tree blossoms, the sweet smelling herbs, and the melodious bird sounds all around her. She wandered deeper and deeper still.

She came upon a beautiful little stream, bubbling over rocks that were covered in moss and little white flowers. These were the Nightshade flowers she was seeking, so she filled her basket. Nearby she also found the mushrooms and wrapped them in her scarf and put those in her basket too.

Dora took out the lunch that Aunt Bruna had made for her. She had brought along her beautiful cup and saucer, and carefully placed them on a flat rock. She poured some water into it, put a piece of German Chocolate Cake on her saucer, and began to eat her lunch.

As she took a sip from her lovely cup, a deer appeared out of the woods and jumped by so closely that it startled Dora, who dropped her cup and knocked over her saucer on the rocks, where they broke into a thousand pieces.

Little Dora burst into tears! When the deer saw her sobbing, he stopped and came back and nuzzled her with his soft, brown muzzle. "Oh, I am so sorry, my dear," said the deer. "What have I done?"

"My cup and saucer are broken. It was from my mother. There are no others like them in the whole wide world!"

"Come with me, my dear," he said with sad, dark eyes. "I will take you to a place where the faerie live. Maybe they can help make things right again." The deer bent down so that Dora could climb up on his back, and he bounded off into the forest, running like the wind. Soon Dora fell asleep, but the deer ran on and on until he reached a part of the woods that no one but animals and faeries knew of.

He set her down near a beautiful waterfall. "Wait here, little one. Soon a water sprite will come and grant you a wish."

The waterfall was full of sparkling crystals. One of the crystals came closer and closer, and closer. It was a water sprite, and it whispered to her, "What is your wish, Little Dora of the Forest?"

"I wish to have my teacup and saucer again."

The sprite led her behind the waterfall. There was a cave there. It was made of crystals and emeralds and rubies, all glittering in the rainbow's beautiful mist.

In the cave there was a stone table filled with precious objects. A necklace made of apple-shaped rubies, a diamond shaped like a prancing unicorn, a cluster of amethyst grapes. Dora's eyes brightened in the sparkle of the beautiful things there.

Then she saw a tiny dish filled with cookies. "Eat Me!" they said. She took one and a little note inside of it said, "Dora, this is your wish . . . close your eyes and turn around once. It will be before you."

Poof! There on the table was a miniature tray with dishes, cups, and saucers, all engraved with the beautiful twisting vines just like the cup and saucer Aunt Bruna had given her. There was a teapot, a sugar bowl, and a creamer, each encircled with a delicate vine, twisting and weaving into a handle of glass leaves and vines. There were seven spoons and forks and knives made out of crystal stones, each twisting like a tiny branch of a tree.

Her eyes could not believe what they were seeing! Suddenly, the rainbow mist surrounded her, and when it cleared she was in Aunt Bruna's kitchen.

"My! Where have you been?" Aunt Bruna cried as she swept her into her arms. "I was so very worried!"

Dora told her aunt the amazing story of what had happened. "Ah," said Aunt Bruna. "That is the same story that your Great, Great Grandmother Theodora told of how she came by the tea set. She spoke of a deer rescuing her from being lost in the forest, and he brought her to the faerie woods. We thought she was telling faeric tales . . . I guess she really was!"

Dora and her Aunt Bruna celebrated. They made a special tea from their herb shelf and ate cake and strudel. They had a grand time at their tea party.

And they are celebrating still.

~Finis~

*In the countryside, the old stories seemed to come
alive around me; the faeries were a tangible aspect
of the landscape, pulses of spirit, emotion, and
light. They "insisted" on taking form under my
pencil, emerging on the page before me cloaked in
archetypal shapes drawn from nature and myth. I'd
attracted their attention, you see, and they hadn't
finished with me yet.*

BRIAN FROUD

Someone to Watch over Me

When it comes to wishes and fairy godmothers, the story of Cinderella often takes center stage. In the next story, by the gentleman who brought you one of the first versions of the Cinderella story, Charles Perrault, we find another giving fairy with the classic elements: the abused but oh-so-fair maiden who is kind of heart, the evil stepsister. The moral of the story: laziness and greed are rewarded with nothing. Or, fairies give to those who deserve it. And not many deserve it.

The Fairy

by Charles Perrault

There was, once upon a time, a widow, who had two daughters. The eldest was so much like her in the face and humour, that whoever looked upon the daughter saw the mother. They were both so disagreeable, and so proud, that there was no living with them. The youngest, who was the very picture of her father, for courtesy and sweetness of temper, was withal one of the most beautiful girls ever seen. As people naturally love their own likeness, this mother even doted on her eldest daughter, and at the same time had a horrible aversion for the youngest. She made her eat in the kitchen, and work continually.

Among other things, this poor child was forced twice a day to draw water above a mile and a half off the house, and bring home a pitcher full of it. One day, as she was at this fountain, there came to her a poor woman, who begged of her to let her drink.

"O ay, with all my heart, Goody," said this pretty maid; and rinsing immediately the pitcher, she took up some water from the clearest place of the fountain, and gave it to her, holding up the pitcher all the while, that she might drink the easier.

The good woman having drank, said to her:

"You are so very pretty, my dear, so good and so mannerly, that I cannot help giving you a gift" (for this was a Fairy, who had taken the form of a poor country-woman, to see how far the civility and good manners of this pretty girl would go). "I will give you for gift," continued the Fairy, "that at every word you speak, there shall come out of your mouth either a flower, or a jewel."

When this pretty girl came home, her mother scolded at her for staying so long at the fountain.

"I beg your pardon, mamma," said the poor girl, "for not making more haste," and, in speaking these words, there came out of her mouth two roses, two pearls, and two diamonds.

"What is this I see?" said her mother quite astonished, "I think I see pearls and diamonds come out of the girl's mouth! How happens this, child?" (This was the first time she ever called her child.)

The poor creature told her frankly all the matter, not without dropping out infinite numbers of diamonds.

"In good faith," cried the mother, "I must send my child thither. Come hither, Fanny, look what comes out of thy sister's mouth when she speaks! Would'st not thou be glad, my dear, to have the same gift given to thee? Thou hast nothing else to do but go and draw water out of the fountain, and when a certain poor woman asks thee to let her drink, to give it her very civilly."

"It would be a very fine sight indeed," said this ill-bred minx, "to see me go draw water!"

"You shall go, hussey," said the mother, "and this minute."

So away she went, but grumbling all the way, taking with her the best silver tankard in the house.

She was no sooner at the fountain, than she saw coming out of the wood a lady most gloriously dressed, who came up to her, and asked to drink. This was, you must know, the very Fairy who appeared to her sister, but had now taken the air and dress of a princess, to see how far this girl's rudeness would go.

"Am I come hither," said the proud, saucy slut, "to serve you with water, pray? I suppose the silver tankard was brought purely for your ladyship, was it? However, you may drink out of it, if you have a fancy."

"You are not over and above mannerly," answered the Fairy, without putting herself in a passion. "Well then, since you have so little breeding, and are so disobliging, I give you for gift, that at every word you speak there shall come out of your mouth a snake or a toad."

So soon as her mother saw her coming, she cried out: "Well, daughter?"

"Well, mother?" answered the pert hussey, throwing out of her mouth two vipers and two toads.

"O mercy!" cried the mother, "what is it I see! O, it is that wretch her sister who has occasioned all this; but she shall pay for it"; and immediately she ran to beat her. The poor child fled away from her and went to hide herself in the forest, not far from thence.

The King's son, then on his return from hunting, met her, and seeing her so very pretty, asked her what she did there alone, and why she cried.

"Alas! sir, my mamma has turned me out of doors."

The King's son, who saw five or six pearls, and as many diamonds, come out of her mouth, desired her to tell him how that happened. She thereupon told him the whole story; and so the King's son fell in love with her; and, considering with himself that such a gift was worth more than any marriage-portion whatsoever in another, conducted her to the palace of the King his father, and there married her.

As for her sister, she made herself so much hated that her own mother turned her off; and the miserable wretch, having wandered about a good while without finding anybody to take her in, went to a corner in the wood and there died.

Fairies, black, grey, green, and white,
You moonshine revellers, and shades of night,
You orphan heirs of fixed destiny,
Attend your office and your quality.

WILLIAM SHAKESPEARE, *THE MERRY WIVES OF WINDSOR*

The Mysterious Fairy Children of Wyken Hall

Wyken Hall in Suffolk, England, is world-renowned for its gardens, part of a 1200-acre farm rich with extensive herb gardens, vineyards, roses, and exquisite topiaries. But to fairy and folklore scholars, it is significant for another reason: a twelfth-century mystery that remains today.

One hot summer day, workers at the farm spotted two children running at the edge of the farm's field. There were no children living on the estate at the time, and so the farmhands followed them. When they caught up with them, they discovered that the children, a boy and a girl, had greenish skin, did not speak English, and seemed highly sensitive to light. The children were frightened and confused, and the laborers brought them at once to their Lord, Richard de Calne, a well-respected and educated knight who lived nearby.

Lord Richard took them in, and as they were clearly starving, offered them food. They refused to eat. He offered them everything available:

vegetables, meat, fresh fruit, fish. It was not until he offered them green beans that they finally ate. In fact, they ate nothing but green beans for months on end. The boy, however, never recovered, and died. The girl regained her health and learned to speak English. When de Calne asked her where she came from, she told him that she was from a place of perpetual twilight. A place where the sun never rises, nor does it set. Across the river from her twilight land, however, is the land of perpetual sunlight. This description fits perfectly with that of Fairyland.

Could these children have been fairies, somehow lost or escaped or possibly tricked from the realm of the fairies? Or were they suffering from chlorosis, a form of anemia caused by malnutrition? Were they victims of neglect and abuse who at last escaped their captor? Chlorosis causes a green tint to the skin and sensitivity to light. Some scholars point out that a story from the same time talks of a greedy man who poisoned his niece and nephew with arsenic and turned them loose in the forest. Were the children his victims?

An Aye for an Aye: The Barter System

Give me an inch
I'll sell you a mile
Give me a shilling
I'll sell you a smile.

RILEY APHERSON, "THE BARTER KING"

The good people may tend toward trickery, but that doesn't meant they aren't fair. In fact, one could argue that a fairy creature's sense of justice might be one of its most endearing (and frustrating) qualities. Leave out your saucer of milk, keep your house tidy, don't steal anything from the Goblin King, and you've got yourself a deal.

The Bwbach, or Boobach, is the good-natured goblin that loves to do favors for the Welsh maid who keeps the house clean. She need only make a good fire and leave out a churn filled with cream on the hearth, along with a dish of cream for the boobach. In the morning she will find the butter already churned for her.

It was once commonplace to add a bed and sometimes other furniture to a home, along with plenty of food, the night before moving in. If, by the next day, the food was not eaten and the crumbs not swept by the door, the house was not safe to move into.

When it comes to fairy tales and bartering, I can think of no better example than the story of *Rumpelstiltskin* as told by the Brothers Grimm.

Rumpelstiltskin

by The Brothers Grimm

There was once a poor Miller who had a beautiful daughter, and one day, having to go to speak with the King, he said, in order to make himself appear of consequence, that he had a daughter who could spin straw into gold. The King was very fond of gold, and thought to himself, "That is an art which would please me very well"; and so he said to the Miller, "If your daughter is so very clever, bring her to the castle in the morning, and I will put her to the proof."

As soon as she arrived the King led her into a chamber which was full of straw; and, giving her a wheel and a reel, he said, "Now set yourself to work, and if you have not spun this straw into gold by an early hour to-morrow, you must die." With these words he shut the room door, and left the maiden alone.

There she sat for a long time, thinking how to save her life; for she understood nothing of the art whereby straw might be spun into gold; and her perplexity increased more and more, till at last she began to weep.

All at once the door opened, and in stepped a little Man, who said, "Good evening, fair maiden; why do you weep so sore?"

"Ah," she replied, "I must spin this straw into gold, and I am sure I do not know how."

The little Man asked, "What will you give me if I spin it for you?"

"My necklace," said the maiden.

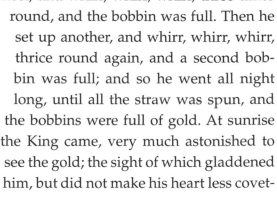

The Dwarf took it, placed himself in front of the wheel, and whirr, whirr, whirr, three times round, and the bobbin was full. Then he set up another, and whirr, whirr, whirr, thrice round again, and a second bobbin was full; and so he went all night long, until all the straw was spun, and the bobbins were full of gold. At sunrise the King came, very much astonished to see the gold; the sight of which gladdened him, but did not make his heart less covetous. He caused the maiden to be led into another room, still larger, full of straw; and then he bade her spin it into gold during the night if she valued her life. The maiden was again quite at a loss what to do; but while she cried the door opened suddenly, as before, and the Dwarf appeared and asked her what she would give him in return for his assistance. "The ring off my finger," she replied.

The little Man took the ring and began to spin at once, and by morning all the straw was changed to glistening gold.

The little Man took the ring and began to spin at once, and by morning all the straw was changed to glistening gold.

The King was rejoiced above measure at the sight of this, but still he was not satisfied, but, leading the maiden into another still larger room, full of straw as the others, he said, "This you must spin during the night; but if you accomplish it you shall be my bride." "For," thought he to himself, "a richer wife thou canst not have in all the world."

When the maiden was left alone, the Dwarf again appeared and asked, for the third time, "What will you give me to do this for you?"

"I have nothing left that I can give you," replied the maiden.

"Then promise me your first-born child if you become Queen," said he.

The Miller's daughter thought, "Who can tell if that will ever happen?" and, ignorant how else to help herself out of her trouble, she promised the Dwarf what he desired; and he immediately set about and finished the spinning. When morning came, and the King found all he had wished for done, he celebrated his wedding, and the Miller's fair daughter became Queen.

The gay times she had at the King's Court caused her to forget that she had made a very foolish promise.

About a year after the marriage, when she had ceased to think about the little Dwarf, she brought a fine child into the world; and, suddenly, soon after its birth, the very man appeared and demanded what she had promised. The frightened Queen offered him all the riches of the kingdom if he would leave her her child; but the Dwarf answered, "No; something human is dearer to me than all the wealth of the world."

The Queen began to weep and groan so much that the Dwarf pitied her, and said, "I will leave you three days to consider; if you in that time discover my name you shall keep your child."

All night long the Queen racked her brains for all the names she could think of, and sent a messenger through the country to collect far and wide any new names. The following morning came the Dwarf, and she began with "Caspar," "Melchior," "Balthassar," and all the odd names she knew; but at each the little Man exclaimed, "That is not my name."

The second day the Queen inquired of all her people for uncommon and curious names, and called the Dwarf "Ribs-of-Beef," "Sheep-shank," "Whalebone," but at each he said, "This is not my name."

The third day the messenger came back and said, "I have not found a single name; but as I came to a

high mountain near the edge of a forest, where foxes and hares say good night to each other, I saw there a little house, and before the door a fire was burning, and round this fire a very curious little Man was dancing on one leg, and shouting:

"To-day I stew, and then I'll bake,
To-morrow I shall the Queen's child take;
Ah! how famous it is that nobody knows
That my name is Rumpelstiltskin."

When the Queen heard this she was very glad, for now she knew the name; and soon after came the Dwarf, and asked, "Now, my lady Queen, what is my name?"

First she said, "Are you called Conrade?" "No."

"Are you called Hal?" "No."

"Are you called Rumpelstiltskin?"

"A witch has told you! a witch has told you!" shrieked the little Man, and stamped his right foot so hard in the ground with rage that he could not draw it out again. Then he took hold of his left leg with both his hands, and pulled away so hard that his right came off in the struggle, and he hopped away howling terribly. And from that day to this the Queen has heard no more of her troublesome visitor.

I believe in everything until it's disproved. So I believe in fairies, the myths, dragons. It all exists, even if it's in your mind. Who's to say that dreams and nightmares aren't as real as the here and now?

JOHN LENNON

Chapter 5
Whoops, There It Is
*How to Enter the Fairy Kingdom
(or How Not To)*

*Finally there are the most hopeless of the lot, those
who claim fairies don't exist at all. They believe all
of life's calamities can be chalked up to one's own
clumsiness or simply to ill luck. This, my friends, is
exactly what the fairies would like us to think.*

REGINALD BAKELEY, FROM *GOBLINPROOFING
ONE'S CHICKEN COOP*

In the wild woods of my childhood, I spent many an
hour seeking out fairy rings. I had been cautioned by
my mother, who was the first to explain to me how
to find a fairy ring, never to disturb one. I could play
near it, I could leave some kind of gift within it, and if
I were very brave I could come down to the meadow

in the moonlight and listen for the song of the fairies. But I was never to touch the mushrooms, never to eat anything the fairies offered (which could appear near or in the ring) and never, under any circumstances, to sit inside the fairy ring. This could result in the fairies carrying me off into Fairyland. And although this land sounded delightful at first thought, every bit of literature I read on the subject seemed to support my mother's reasons: for one thing, you had to abide by the fairy rules (no kid wants to hear there's a place with even more rules than they currently have to follow). Also, fairies like to constantly test and trick you, so that you could never really relax in Fairyland. And, for another thing, you almost certainly would never come back, especially if you ate so much as a crumb or drank so much as a thimbleful.

Circles, in all of their obvious symbolism, have long been associated with gateways into the magical kingdom. In Wales, circles in the grass of green fields are called fairy rings. Ditto for stone circles, small piles of stones and little mounds, perfectly formed. In his book on Irish fairy and folklore, William Butler Yeats describes the forts of ancient Celts as being taken over by the wee folk:

> Forts, otherwise raths or royalties, are circular ditches enclosing a little field, where, in most cases, if you dig down you come to stone chambers, their bee-hive roofs and walls made of unmortared stone. In these little fields the ancient Celts fortified themselves and their cattle, in winter retreating into the stone chambers, where also they were buried. The people call them Dane's forts, from a

misunderstanding of the word Dan⁻an (Tuath-de-Dan⁻an). The fairies have taken up their abode therein, guarding them from all disturbance. Whoever roots them up soon finds his cattle falling sick, or his family or himself. Near the raths are sometimes found flint arrowheads; these are called "fairy darts," and are supposed to have been flung by the fairies, when angry, at men or cattle.

Many believe the circles are formed by the dancing fairies themselves, others just that they dance within. The sound of their laughter, music, and song creates a din so lulling that it isn't long before the wayward soul is drawn to the party. Not all people can see the fairy folk, and just as some people can see ghosts but not hear them, or hear them but not see them, so too happens with fairies. In William Wirt Sikes' *British Goblins*, we hear of the Dancing Place of the Goblin. He describes a magical yew tree that grows "exactly in the middle of the forest." This particular yew tree is the spot where two farmhands, Tom and Iago, were working in the Forest of the Yew on one warm afternoon when a great mist overtook the sky and made them think it sunset. As they headed home, thinking their workday over as it was getting dark, they came upon the yew tree in the middle of the forest and from it came a great light, making them think it was actually still the peak of day. They decided not to head home so early after all, and instead agreed it was best to rest there. They fell asleep. When Tom awoke, he found his companion gone. Assuming his pal had simply headed home, he also made his way back to the village. The

next day Iago did not show up for work, and a great search went underway. During the search, Tom admitted they had fallen asleep in the fairy ring. After many days of searching, Tom went to a conjurer for advice.

The conjurer told him to wait exactly one year to the day that Iago disappeared, and then go back to the yew in the middle of the forest, and lie down near the fairy ring (being careful not to step inside the fairy ring) and wait. His friend would soon come out, dancing with the goblins, and Tom was to snatch him and run away. Some time passed and at last the day came. Tom followed the instructions, and just as the conjure-woman had said. Iago appeared, dancing in the ring, and Tom snatched him up. Iago looked very pale and skeletal, for he had not eaten any real food for a year and did not know any time had passed.

Were my mother's words of warning, like those passed down over centuries to other children, just a way to keep me from straying too far into the woods, getting lost and whisked away to the den of some wild animal? Or perhaps a way to prevent unknown poisons—tempting shiny red berries and meaty looking mushrooms—from ending up in the mouths of babes? Maybe. But I wasn't going to risk it then and I certainly wouldn't now. Like Tom, I prefer to remain at the fairy ring's edge.

The following story, which has many variations, is of Scottish origin and is taken from the volume of *English Fairy Tales*, edited by Joseph Jacobs circa 1890. In it, we learn the secrets to not only entering the Kingdom of Fairy (round the church widdershins, or counterclockwise, it seems is all it takes) but also how to get back out. Note the chant, which you will no doubt recognize from Jack and the Beanstalk, "Fee, fi, fo, fum." It is also no accident that in this Anglicized version, the Church serves as the gateway (it is still commonly believed that churches throughout England and Ireland are built on top of sacred sites of the Celts and pagan people) and the "Christian man" sniffed out by the dreaded bogey is the persecuted hero. Keep this one handy should you ever "accidentally" find yourself asleep on a fairy mound or walking the "wrong way" around a portal to the fairy realm.

Childe Rowland

by Joseph Jacobs, Ed.

Childe Rowland and his brothers twain
Were playing at the ball,
And there was their sister Burd Ellen
In the midst, among them all.
Childe Rowland kicked it with his foot
And caught it with his knee;
At last as he plunged among them all
O'er the church he made it flee.
Burd Ellen round about the aisle
To seek the ball is gone,
But long they waited, and longer still,
And she came not back again.
They sought her east, they sought her west,
They sought her up and down,
And woe were the hearts of those brethren,
For she was not to be found.

So at last her eldest brother went to the Warlock Merlin and told him all the case, and asked him if he knew where Burd Ellen was. "The fair Burd Ellen," said the Warlock Merlin, "must have been carried off by the fairies, because she went round the church 'wider shins'— the opposite way to the sun. She is now in the Dark Tower of the King of Elfland; it would take the boldest knight in Christendom to bring her back."

"If it is possible to bring her back," said her brother, "I'll do it, or perish in the attempt."

"Possible it is," said the Warlock Merlin, "but woe to the man or mother's son that attempts it, if he is not well taught beforehand what he is to do."

The eldest brother of Burd Ellen was not to be put off, by any fear of danger, from attempting to get her back, so he begged the Warlock Merlin to tell him what he should do, and what he should not do, in going to seek his sister. And after he had been taught, and had repeated his lesson, he set out for Elfland.

But long they waited, and longer
    still,
With doubt and muckle pain,
But woe were the hearts of his
    brethren,
For he came not back again.

Then the second brother got tired and sick of waiting, and he went to the Warlock Merlin and asked him the same as his brother. So he set out to find Burd Ellen.

But long they waited, and longer still,
With muckle doubt and pain,
And woe were his mother's and brother's
    heart,
For he came not back again.

And when they had waited and waited a good long time, Childe Rowland, the youngest of Burd Ellen's brothers, wished to go, and went to his mother, the good queen, to ask her to let him go. But she would not at first, for he was the last of her children she now had, and if he was lost, all would be lost. But he begged, and he begged, till at last the good queen let him go, and gave him his father's good brand that never struck in vain. And as she girt it round his waist, she said the spell that would give it victory.

So Childe Rowland said good-bye to the good queen, his mother, and went to the cave of the Warlock Merlin. "Once more, and but once more," he said to the Warlock, "tell how man or mother's son may rescue Burd Ellen and her brothers twain."

"Well, my son," said the Warlock Merlin, "there are but two things, simple they may seem, but hard they are to do. One thing to do, and one thing not to do. And the thing to do is this: after you have entered the land of Fairy, whoever speaks to you, till you meet the Burd Ellen, you must out with your father's brand and off with their head." "And what you've not to do is this: bite no bit, and drink no drop, however hungry or thirsty you be; drink a drop, or bite a bit, while in Elfland you be and never will you see Middle Earth again."

"And what you've not to do is this: bite no bit, and drink no drop, however hungry or thirsty you be; drink a drop, or bite a bit, while in Elfland you be and never will you see Middle Earth again."

So Childe Rowland said the two things over and over again, till he knew them by heart, and he thanked the Warlock Merlin and went on his way. And he went along, and along, and along, and still further along, till he came to the horse-herd of the King of Elfland feeding his horses. These he knew by their fiery eyes, and knew that he was at last in the land of Fairy. "Canst thou tell me," said Childe Rowland to the horse-herd, "where the King of Elfland's Dark Tower is?" "I cannot tell thee," said the horse-herd, "but go on a little further and thou wilt come to the cow-herd, and he, maybe, can tell thee."

Then, without a word more, Childe Rowland drew the good brand that never struck in vain, and off went the horse-herd's head, and Childe Rowland went on further, till he came to the cow-herd, and asked him the same question. "I can't tell thee," said he, "but go on a little farther, and thou wilt come to the hen-wife, and she is sure to know." Then Childe Rowland out with his good brand, that never struck in vain, and off went the cow-herd's head. And he went on a little further, till he came to an old woman in a grey cloak, and he asked her if she knew where the Dark Tower of the King of Elfland was. "Go on a little further," said the hen-wife, "till you come to a round green hill, surrounded with terrace-rings, from the bottom to the top; go round it three times, widdershins, and each time say:

Open, door! open, door!
And let me come in.

and the third time the door will open, and you may go in." And Childe Rowland was just going on, when he remembered what he had to do; so he out with the good brand, that never struck in vain, and off went the hen-wife's head.

Then he went on, and on, and on, till he came to the round green hill with the terrace-rings from top to bottom, and he went round it three times, widdershins, saying each time:

Open, door! open, door!
And let me come in.

And the third time the door did open, and he went in, and it closed with a click, and Childe Rowland was left in the dark.

It was not exactly dark, but a kind of twilight or gloaming. There were neither windows nor candles, and he could not make out where the twilight came from, if not through the walls and roof. These were rough arches made of a transparent rock, incrusted with sheepsilver and rock spar, and other bright stones. But though it was rock, the air was quite warm, as it always is in Elfland. So he went through this passage till at last he came to two wide and high folding-doors which stood ajar. And when he opened them, there he saw a most wonderful and glorious sight. A large and spacious hall, so large that it seemed to be as long, and as broad, as the green hill itself. The roof was supported by fine pillars, so large and lofty, that the pillars of a cathedral were as nothing to them. They were all of gold and silver, with fretted work, and between them and around them, wreaths of flowers, composed of what do you think? Why, of diamonds and emeralds, and all manner of precious stones. And the very key-stones of the arches had for ornaments clusters of diamonds and rubies, and pearls, and other precious stones. And all these arches met in the middle of the roof, and just there, hung by a gold chain, an immense lamp made out of one big pearl hollowed out and quite transparent. And in the middle of this was a big, huge carbuncle, which kept spinning round and round, and this was what gave light by its rays to the whole hall, which seemed as if the setting sun was shining on it.

The hall was furnished in a manner equally grand, and at one end of it was a glorious couch of velvet,

silk and gold, and there sate Burd Ellen, combing her golden hair with a silver comb. And when she saw Childe Rowland she stood up and said:

> *"God pity ye, poor luckless fool,*
> *   What have ye here to do?*
> *Hear ye this, my youngest brother,*
> *   Why didn't ye bide at home?*
> *Had you a hundred thousand lives*
> *   Ye couldn't spare any a one.*
> *But sit ye down; but woe, O, woe,*
> *   That ever ye were born,*
> *For come the King of Elfland in,*
> *   Your fortune is forlorn."*

Then they sate down together, and Childe Rowland told her all that he had done, and she told him how their two brothers had reached the Dark Tower, but had

been enchanted by the King of Elfland, and lay there entombed as if dead. And then after they had talked a little longer Childe Rowland began to feel hungry from his long travels, and told his sister Burd Ellen how hungry he was and asked for some food, forgetting all about the Warlock Merlin's warning.

Burd Ellen looked at Childe Rowland sadly, and shook her head, but she was under a spell, and could not warn him. So she rose up, and went out, and soon brought back a golden basin full of bread and milk. Childe Rowland was just going to raise it to his lips, when he looked at his sister and remembered why he had come all that way.

So he dashed the bowl to the ground, and said: "Not a sup will I swallow, nor a bit will I bite, till Burd Ellen is set free."

So he dashed the bowl to the ground, and said: "Not a sup will I swallow, nor a bit will I bite, till Burd Ellen is set free."

Just at that moment they heard the noise of someone approaching, and a loud voice was heard saying:

"Fee, fi, fo, fum,
I smell the blood of a Christian
man,
Be he dead, be he living, with
my brand,
I'll dash his brains from his
brain-pan."

And then the folding-doors of the hall were burst open, and the King of Elfland rushed in.

"Strike then, Bogle, if thou darest," shouted out Childe Rowland, and rushed to meet him with his good brand that never yet did fail. They fought, and they fought, and they fought, till Childe Rowland beat the King of Elfland down on to his knees, and caused him to yield and beg for mercy. "I grant thee mercy," said Childe Rowland, "release my sister from thy spells and raise my brothers to life, and let us all go free, and thou shalt be spared."

"I agree," said the Elfin King, and rising up he went to a chest from which he took a phial filled with a blood-red liquor. With this he anointed the ears, eyelids, nostrils, lips, and finger-tips, of the two brothers, and they sprang at once into life, and declared that their souls had been away, but had now returned. The Elfin king then said some words to Burd Ellen, and she was disenchanted, and they all four passed out of the hall,

through the long passage, and turned their back on the Dark Tower, never to return again. And they reached home, and the good queen, their mother, and Burd Ellen never went round a church widdershins again.

Feeling Fae?

If you love fairies and want to go beyond the pages of a book, get thee to FaerieCon. This international convention takes place in the Hunt Valley in Maryland and includes guest speakers and musical acts, an elaborate masquerade ball, hundreds of vendors with costumes, fairy-themed goods, magical items, and fairy-art, plus the ultimate excuse to wear a cloak in public. *www.faeriecon.com*

Also in Maryland, you can take part in the Maryland Faerie Festival, held each summer in Darlington. Immerse yourself in folklore, outdoor education and nature play, fairy artists, merchants, and entertainment. *marylandfaerie festival.org*

The "World's Largest Fairy Festival" takes place in Oregon in early September each year. Faerieworlds has been described as "Bonaroo for Middle Earth" and features musical acts, vendors, and camping. *faerieworlds.com*

What Not to Wear: Fairy Ointment

In addition to fairy rings, one must be careful not to fall prey to the fairies' more domestic temptations. Yeats recounts a story from a humble midwife who was asked by a strange man (of course) to come to his home to help birth a child. The woman made her way to a castle she did not know and, as was her profession, helped to birth the child. When the babe was born, the midwife noticed that all of the women there put their hands in a bowl of water and then rubbed their eyes. And so the midwife did the same, rubbing just one of her eyes. She was paid well and sent home, and she thought of it no more. Later, the midwife was at a local fair and recognized some of the women from the castle who had been present at the birth. She approached them in a friendly manner and asked after the health of the baby. One of the women looked at her and said, "How do you see us?" The midwife said she could only see them from one eye. The fairy woman then blew her breath on that eye and declared the old midwife would ne'er see them again. And so she was blind ever after in that eye.

"Fairy Ointment" tells a very similar story in rich detail, although in this version the nursemaid appears less innocent than in the Yeats version.

Fairy Ointment

by Joseph Jacobs, Ed.

Dame Goody was a nurse that looked after sick people, and minded babies. One night she was woke up at midnight, and when she went downstairs, she saw a strange squinny-eyed, little ugly old fellow, who asked her to come to his wife who was too ill to mind her baby. Dame Goody didn't like the look of the old fellow, but business is business; so she popped on her things, and went down to him. And when she got down to him, he whisked her up on to a large coal-black horse with fiery eyes, that stood at the door; and soon they were going at a rare pace, Dame Goody holding on to the old fellow like grim death.

They rode, and they rode, till at last they stopped before a cottage door. So they got down and went in and found the good woman abed with the children playing about; and the babe, a fine bouncing boy, beside her.

Dame Goody took the babe, which was as fine a baby boy as you'd wish to see. The mother, when she handed the baby to Dame Goody to mind, gave her a box of ointment, and told her to stroke the baby's eyes with it as soon as it opened them. After a while it began to open its eyes. Dame Goody saw that it had squinny eyes just like its father. So she took the box of ointment and stroked its two eyelids with it. But she couldn't help wondering what it was for, as she had never seen such a thing done before. So she looked to see if the others were looking, and, when they were not noticing she stroked her own right eyelid with the ointment.

No sooner had she done so, than everything seemed changed about her. The cottage became elegantly furnished. The mother in the bed was a beautiful lady, dressed up in white silk. The little baby was still more beautiful than before, and its clothes were made of a sort of silvery gauze. Its little brothers and sisters around the bed were flat-nosed imps with pointed ears, who made faces at one another, and scratched their polls. Sometimes they would pull the sick lady's ears

with their long and hairy paws. In fact, they were up to all kinds of mischief; and Dame Goody knew that she had got into a house of pixies. But she said nothing to nobody, and as soon as the lady was well enough to mind the baby, she asked the old fellow to take her back home. So he came round to the door with the coal-black horse with eyes of fire, and off they went as fast as before, or perhaps a little faster, till they came to Dame Goody's cottage, where the squinny-eyed old fellow lifted her down and left her, thanking her civilly enough, and paying her more than she had ever been paid before for such service.

Now next day happened to be market-day, and as Dame Goody had been away from home, she wanted many things in the house, and trudged off to get them at the market. As she was buying the things she wanted, who should she see but the squinny-eyed old fellow who had taken her on the coal-black horse. And what do you think he was doing? Why he went about from stall to stall taking up things from each, here some fruit, and there some eggs, and so on; and no one seemed to take any notice.

Now Dame Goody did not think it her business to interfere, but she thought she ought not to let so good a customer pass without speaking. So she ups to him and bobs a curtsey and said: "Gooden, sir, I hopes as how your good lady and the little one are as well as—"

But she couldn't finish what she was a-saying, for the funny old fellow started back in surprise, and he says to her, says he: "What! do you see me today?"

"See you," says she, "why, of course I do, as plain as the sun in the skies, and what's more," says she, "I see you are busy too, into the bargain."

"Ah, you see too much," said he; "now, pray, with which eye do you see all this?"

"With the right eye to be sure," said she, as proud as can be to find him out.

"The ointment! The ointment!" cried the old pixy thief. "Take that for meddling with what don't concern you: you shall see me no more." And with that he struck her on her right eye, and she couldn't see him any more; and, what was worse, she was blind on the right side from that hour till the day of her death.

Food, after it has been put out at night for the fairies, is not allowed to be eaten afterwards by man or beast, not even by pigs. Such food is said to have no real substance left in it, and to let anything eat it wouldn't be thought of. The underlying idea seems to be that the fairies extract the spiritual essence from food offered to them, leaving behind the grosser elements.

W. Y. EVANS-WENTZ, FROM *THE FAIRY-FAITH
IN CELTIC COUNTRIES*

Goodbye Is Not Forever

I take my leave of you now, and it is not without apology. No, I am not sorry for the nightmares these pages may cause, nor for the fevers that may come as you begin your own hunt for life among the craggy edges and tattered fields. If you should be more cautious walking home half-drunk or walk the long way round the bog, this is probably for the best. My apologies are for not being able to warn you completely: There are many walking, slinking, slithering, sneaking beings that did not make their way into these pages (or ended up on the cutting room floor). The tap-tapping sounds and the unexplained missing items, the certainty that someone just dashed across the lawn, it could be nothing at all. It could be nothing, but we both know that isn't true. It is something. I'm afraid you are on your own to discover just exactly what.

IN UNDYING FREAKITUDE,
VARLA

The End

For every child should understand
That letters from the first were planned
To guide us into Fairy Land.

ANDREW LANG

Acknowledgments

A book such as this could not be possible were it not for the sleepless nights caused by the stories, books, ideas, and legends shared with me. My dearest friends Alix, Madeleine, Mischa, Anna, Stacey, Maureen, Cristina, Julie, Sumita and Clare: your laughter during ladies' nights, drunken clothing swaps, and long phone calls ring out into the blackness of midnight and keep me going. Elizabeth Jens, I am still convinced you are not of this realm and all who view your beauty will agree. Olaf, you are the luckiest man alive. Lucy Lee and Lorian, your expertise is always welcome and I hope you read this with the lights on. To Chris Ward and Gem Blade, may the blessings of the Fairy Queen forever enchant your home and your marriage. To Sara, thank you for reading a first draft, getting scared, and making me feel less crazy. To Chris H. and Jen, not a day goes by that I don't think of you and all the wicked fun we've had. Huge thanks to my super supportive family, especially my nieces and nephews: Emma, Ida, Aurora, Jacob, Andy III, Sabrina, Corrine, Phillip, Natalie, and Luke, you are the whole reason I wrote this book. To my brother Andy II and his beautiful wife, Sue: fairy photo-shoot this summer! To Wendy the Witch, I swear I did see a leprechaun down at Oregon Creek. To Ethan, who definitely knows a good garden gnome when he sees one; to my sisters Debbie, Dina, and Trevisa, thank you

for coaching me through the perils of life and writing; and to my brother Donn, who probably doesn't believe a word of this book but loves me anyway. (PS: Amber, we're all on to you!) Triple thanks to my mom, the believer, and my dad, the realist, who balance out the worlds of Twilight and Perpetual Sun. To my beloved little personal imp, Henrik, and to KRP, you have my undying love (plus you can spend my royalty checks). Grateful acknowledgement to Dark Horse Rosé, without whom most of this writing would not be possible.

Thank you to my editor Judika Illes, who is one of my favorite authors, too, so that works out well! To Jane Hagaman for sheparding the manuscript and the wonderful Julia Campbell for graciously pointing out the gaps. To Michael Kerber, who benefits from the luck of the fae most days (but don't tell his wife). To publisher emeritus of Weiser, Jan Johnson, who always, always believed in me and who never, ever, ever gives up. Special thanks to Sylvia Hopkins for helping me make sense of things and to the incredible sprite that is Bonni Hamilton. If you don't know her, you should. Big shout-out to Eryn Carter for all of her publicity aid and absolute kindness and Mike Conlon for (hopefully) securing flaps, matte finish, or some other bell or whistle for this book. And Jim Warner, who knows a good thing when he sees it. To the entire staff at Red Wheel/ Weiser Books, including Hilary, Sarah, and Angie, you are all incredible and I miss you. (Except for Greg Brandenburgh: I know where you live!!) And in loving memory of Meg Richardson: this one's for you!

Bibliography

The following books are in the public domain and were viewed and read thanks to the amazing Project Gutenberg. In some cases exact names of publishers or publication dates were not available on the copyright page (or the copyright page was missing). Every attempt has been made to credit those whose extensive work on the subject of fairies and folklore, largely during the Victorian era, remains as some of the only written accounts of a time and a place that have quickly faded from memory. I am exceedingly grateful that so many obscure volumes of otherwise-forgotten lore have been made available to the public, for even a book collector like myself will find it hard to locate some of these on common shelves. I have made a donation to Project

Gutenberg and encourage you to explore the site and make one yourself.

Alcott, Louisa May. *Flower Fables*. Boston, 1894.

Beston, Henry. *The Firelight Fairy Book*. Boston: Little, Brown & Company, 1919.

Croker, T. Crofton. *Fairy Legends and Traditions of the South of Ireland*. Philadelphia: Lea and Blanchard, 1844.

Evans-Wentz, W. Y. *The Fairy-Faith in Celtic Countries*. Oxford University Press. London: 1911.

Graves, Perceval Alfred, Ed. *The Irish Fairy Book.*

Grierson, Elizabeth W. *The Scottish Fairy Book*. Philadelphia: J. B. Lippincott Company

Griffis, William Elliot. *Welsh Fairy Tales*. 1921.

Guiney, Louise Imogen. *Brownies and Bogles*. Boston: D. Lothrop Co., 1888.

Jacobs, Joseph, Ed. *English Fairy Tales*. London, c. 1890.

Jacobs, Joseph, Ed. *Indian Fairy Tales*. London, 1892.

Keightley, Thomas. *The Fairy Mythology*. London: George Bell & Sons, 1892.

Lang, Jean (Mrs. John Lang). *A Book of Myths*. New York: G. P. Putnam, 1915.

Mabie, Hamilton Wright. *Legends Every Child Should Know*. 1905.

McAnally (Jr.), D. R., *Irish Wonders*. New York: Weathervane. 1888.

Middleton, Tom. *Legends of Longendale*. Cheshire, England: Clarendon Press. 1906.

Ozaki, Yei Theodora. *Japanese Fairy Tales.* 1908.

Sikes, William Wirt. *British Goblins: Welsh Folk-Lore, Fairy Mythology, Legends and Traditions.* London: Sampson Low, Marston, Searle & Rivington, 1880.

Stroebe, Clara, Ed. *The Norwegian Fairy Book*. New York: Frederick A. Stokes, 1922.

Additional sources

Andersen, Hans Christian. *Andersen's Fairy Tales*. New York: A. L. Burt Company.

Bakeley, Reginald. *Goblinproofing One's Chicken Coop: And Other Practical Advice in Our Campaign against the Fairy Kingdom.* San Francisco: Conari Press, 2012.

Barrie, James M. *Peter Pan.* New York: Sterling, 2009.

Buchanan, Dougal, compiled by. *Gaelic-English, English-Gaelic Dictionary.* New Lanark, Scotland: Geddes & Grosset Ltd., 1998

Buckland, Raymond. *The Weiser Field Guide to Ghosts*. San Francisco: Weiser Books, 2009.

Desai, A. R. *Rural Sociology in India*. Bombay: Popular Prakashan, 1969 via googlebooks, Feb./Mar. 2016, 234. *https://books.google.com/books/about/Rural_Sociology_in_India.html?id=MKWWu7TLAb8C*

Eason, Cassandra. *A Complete Guide to Faeries & Magical Beings*. York Beach, ME: Weiser, 2002.

Froud, Brian. *Fairies*. New York: Bantam, 1976.

Grimm, Jacob and Wilhelm. *The Complete Grimm's Fairy Tales: with intro. by Padraic Colum and commentary by Joseph Campbell*. New York: Pantheon, 1944 and 1976.

Guetebier, Amber, and Brenda Knight. *The Poetry Oracle*. San Francisco: CCC Publications, 2008.

Hamilton, John. *Elves and Fairies.* Edina, MN: ABDO Publishing, 2005.

———. *Goblins and Trolls*. Edina, MN: ABDO Publishing, 2005.

Hawken, Paul. *The Magic of Findhorn*. New York: Harper & Row, 1975.

Hunt, Robert. *Cornish Legends*. Cornwall, England: Tor Mark Press, 1990.

Kirk, Robert. *The Secret Commonwealth of Elves, Fauns and Fairies*. New York: NYRB, 2007.

Lang, Andrew, Ed. *The Yellow Fairy Book**. New York: Dover, 1966.

Pepper, Elizabeth, and Barbara Stacy. *The Little Book of Magical Creatures*. Newport, RI: Witches Almanac, 2009.

Perrault, Charles. *The Fairy Tales of Charles Perrault*. London: George Hathrup & Co., 1922.

Shakespear, John. *A Dictionary, Hindūstānī and English, and English and Hindūstānī*. London: Richardson Bros., 1849. Accessed via googlebooks Feb. 2016 *https://books.google.com/books?id=cQFfAAAAcAAJ&dq=A+Dictionary,+Hind%C5%ABst%C4%81n%C4%AB+and+English&*

Sorenson-Winther, Rebecca. "10 Creatures in Scandinavia Folklore" Listverse, Oct. 2012, accessed Jan.-Feb. 2016. *http://listverse.com/2012/10/15/10-creatures-in-scandinavian-folklore/*

---

* All of the fairy books by Andrew Lang, such as *The Red Fairy Book*, *The Blue Fairy Book*, *The Pink Fairy Book*, etc., are in the public domain and thus available for free on *Gutenberg.org*. Nonetheless, there is something delightful about having this collection of books on your shelf and Dover does an excellent job of publishing all (or nearly all) of them.

Ventura, Varla. *Among the Mermaids.* San Francisco: Weiser Books, 2013.

―――. *Banshees, Werewolves, Vampires, and Other Creatures of the Night.* San Francisco: Weiser Books, 2013.

Wilde, Lady. *Irish Cures, Mystic Charms & Superstitions.* New York: Sterling, 1991.

"Wyken Hall." *Mysteries at the Castle.* Travel Channel, first aired Jan. 20, 2015.

Yeats, W. B. *Fairy and Folk Tales of Ireland*.* New York: Simon & Schuster, 1996.

―――. *Irish Fairy Tales.* London: T. Fisher Unwin, 1892.

Websites

www.ancestry.com

www.faeriecon.com

faeryfolklorist.blogspot.com

www.irishcentral.com

www.orionfoxwood.com

---

* This is a hardcover edition of the public domain *Fairy and Folk Tales of the Irish Peasantry*, compiled by Yeats in 1889.

To Our Readers

Weiser Books, an imprint of Red Wheel/Weiser, publishes books across the entire spectrum of occult, esoteric, speculative, and New Age subjects. Our mission is to publish quality books that will make a difference in people's lives without advocating any one particular path or field of study. We value the integrity, originality, and depth of knowledge of our authors.

Our readers are our most important resource, and we appreciate your input, suggestions, and ideas about what you would like to see published.

Visit our website at *www.redwheelweiser.com* to learn about our upcoming books and free downloads, and be sure to go to *www.redwheelweiser.com/newsletter* to sign up for newsletters and exclusive offers.

You can also contact us at *info@rwwbooks.com* or at

Red Wheel/Weiser, LLC
65 Parker Street, Suite 7
Newburyport, MA 01950